the bead seller

Sweetfern Harbor Mystery - 11

wendy meadows

❋ Created with Vellum

chapter one

Phyllis kissed her husband goodbye for the day and joined Brenda for their early morning coffee. It was a busy day in the bed and breakfast, but Brenda and her head housekeeper started every day together in order to plan the work ahead. Every room must be perfect in Sheffield Bed and Breakfast to welcome the acting troupe soon to arrive. Phyllis told Brenda that as soon as they had their morning chat, she would do a last dusting in the sitting room. Anticipation ran high in town and at the bed and breakfast about the incoming guests, because an early summer theatre performance was bound to attract many tourists to the town. The women took their last sips of coffee and Phyllis bustled off to the dusting and to inspect the guest rooms. Brenda remembered she needed to meet with her chef that morning and headed back to the spacious kitchen in the rear of the house.

At the front desk, the young reservationist, Allie, took one last look at the reservation roster. She had a few spare minutes, so she quickly looked up a few of the names online, wondering if any of them were famous actors. She gasped and called out to Phyllis just as she was passing by with an armful of cleaning supplies.

"Phyllis, look at this! I just discovered that one of our guests is a psychic." The young reservationist's eyes sparkled. "I can't believe it. I'll call my mother right away. I know we'll have readings before this long weekend ends."

Phyllis set her duster down on the nearby hall table. "Who is it?"

"Her name is Tiana Lockser. I've never heard of her, but it's exciting to know someone like that will be a guest here." Allie quickly called her mother. Hope Williams owned Sweet Treats in downtown Sweetfern Harbor.

"When is she arriving?" Hope asked. "I can't believe a famous psychic is actually coming to our town." She went on to explain she had heard of the woman but didn't know much about her.

Allie told her mother that Tiana was scheduled to arrive before dinnertime that evening. "Come over tomorrow morning after breakfast. Maybe we can get a reading from her right away."

Brenda came from the kitchen area. She stopped in the passageway and listened to the excited voices of her two most trustworthy employees. She already knew a psychic was booked into her bed and breakfast but had opted not to tell Allie just yet, knowing how excitable the young girl could be. Now that everything was in order to receive their next guests, she was excited to discuss it, however, with both Allie and Phyllis. She smiled to herself when she noted the anticipation in their eyes.

"I knew to expect her." Brenda explained she wanted everything ready before she let Allie know. "I planned to tell you before Tiana arrived. But I don't think we should expect her to work while she is here. She may be coming to get away from that sort of thing."

Allie's face fell but only for a split second. "If she wants to give readings, will you encourage her?"

"I'll allow it, but I don't know about outright encouraging it. Once she is settled in, maybe you can ask her in private. I'm sure your mother will want to know." Allie blushed and explained she had already telephoned her mother.

Brenda was on the fence when it came to psychics and mediums. She didn't know if they were for real or simply out to make a buck for notoriety. With the acting troupe coming in, she worried about the mix of the two.

Allie explained that her father, David Williams, did not believe mediums were for real and tried to discourage his wife and daughter from believing in them in the past. It was a fruitless effort. He had no idea at the moment that a psychic was expected at Sheffield Bed and Breakfast. Mother and daughter had agreed to avoid telling him.

The three women looked up when Mac Rivers came through the back entrance and into the foyer. He asked about the excitement after he kissed his wife. The detective's gaze lingered on Brenda's face before he turned to Allie, who told him about the guest who had caught their attention.

"Do you believe in psychics, Mac?" Phyllis asked.

"I don't know. I do find them interesting at times and at other times I think they are all shams to deceive and upset people. I have to admit that we used one on a difficult case about seven years ago in the department." All eyes were on the detective. "She turned out to be helpful in that she pinpointed where the crime occurred, which we didn't know at the time. Later, we found she had been right. She gave a vague description of the perpetrator. Some of her information helped but in the long run it was good detective work on the part of the force that solved the crime."

Brenda made a mental note to ask for more details when they were alone. She was a sleuth in her own right and often worked on cases with the Sweetfern Harbor Police Department. Chief Bob Ingram had been so impressed with her ability to solve crimes that he had recently made her part of the official team. While she focused on Sheffield Bed and Breakfast much of the time, when a crime required extra investigative work, she was always called in to assist.

"Let's all go in to the dining room and have coffee. I want to discuss the guests coming and generally what we should expect." Brenda asked Phyllis to gather the other employees.

They all followed Brenda, except for Mac, who told her he brought work home with him—some files to look into in the peace and quiet of their home. He walked out the back door and along the pathway to the cottage built for him and Brenda. The gardener's work looked stunning, with the flowering shrubbery and garden beds of roses and lilies bordering the lawns. A vegetable garden thrived behind a tidy white fence at the back edge of the property. Mac found the scene cleared his mind. Brenda's ideas for their home in the renovated cottage perfectly matched the architecture of the 1890s Queen Anne bed and breakfast. Despite being almost completely renovated top to bottom, the smaller structure looked as if it had been built in the same era as the mansion.

Morgan Graber, Brenda's chef, brought coffee and tea to the employees and sat down to join them. Brenda glanced twice at the woman's face. She and Phyllis exchanged glances.

"Are you all right, Morgan?" Brenda asked. "You seem a little distracted."

Morgan blushed and assured them she was just fine. "I'll tell you what is going on later, but it has nothing to do with the bed and breakfast."

The others chuckled simultaneously. Everyone knew the chef and Brenda's father had big plans. Brenda hoped Tim Sheffield and Morgan had finally set a date for their wedding. She, Phyllis and Allie were ready for the word. They made big plans for the celebration.

"We'll wait, but you two can't keep us in suspense like this much longer." Brenda opened her notebook. "I know you've all heard that we'll have a psychic in the bed and breakfast. As for the other guests, most of them are with the acting troupe. The play to be performed in Sweetfern Harbor's outdoor theatre is called "Mystery Along the Nile." It is based on Agatha Christie's famous one called "Murder on the Nile." There are variations from the original, of course. As I understand it, a couple of the actors who are coming aspire to leading roles one day. Kathryn Parker is one of them. She has never achieved much notable fame, though she is apparently a good actress. Then there is Keith Moore, an older actor who always plays minor roles."

"How do you know so much about them?" Allie asked.

"William has told me a little about the cast. He said Kelly Reed, the lead actress, is very well known in theatre circles in New York. Her co-star Scott Wilson is also talented. As you know, William is the one who continues to bring excellent talent up to our historic town. He hasn't disappointed us this time, it seems." All eyes shifted to Phyllis Pendleton. "You'll have to thank your husband again, Phyllis."

Phyllis waved her hand. "He doesn't want thanks. All of this is right up his alley, and he loves every minute of it."

Brenda continued to discuss the other guests. A physician who traveled with the troupe was also a guest. Dr. Arthur Walker gave up a lucrative career in New York to join the crew on the road. He was divorced and had no children. His grueling and successful practice became too much for him. According to William, Dr. Walker loved traveling with the group and made sure they all maintained good health.

"I noticed a Rocky Masters on the list," Allie said. "Do you know anything about him?"

Brenda looked at Morgan. "He is a former chef in an upscale restaurant. In fact, he rose to own the place. Dr. Walker, a good friend of his, convinced him to come along with them and prepare nutritious meals when possible. I have no idea why he has taken time off to do something like that, but he has. Rocky has assured William he has no intentions of invading our kitchen unless invited to do so.

You can determine that, Morgan, but I believe that tells us he wants a break." Brenda continued to discuss others. Jeffery Johnson would accompany the psychic, as was his norm, being some sort of companion or assistant to her. "That's all I know for the moment. Let's all return to our tasks now. I want to thank everyone for the good work you do here."

Several of the housekeepers chattered in the hallway after the meeting. Allie joined them, and the subject centered on the psychic.

"We may have time for a stroll downtown, Phyllis, if you want to come along." Brenda took one last look around. Phyllis was ready to get out of the bed and breakfast for a while. Both expected the buzz around Sweetfern Harbor to be about the theatre troupe coming into town.

They headed for the main street and stopped first to say hello to Jenny Jones, Brenda's step-daughter. Jenny's Blossoms displayed a fetching scene in the wide window.

"Jenny's done it again," Phyllis commented. Brenda agreed. They admired the spray of lilies in the background. Whimsical figures scattered among a meadow scene.

Jenny bent over a large container of newly-arrived flowers and placed them into the refrigerator. Brenda caught her breath when she saw the younger woman's face. Jenny glowed. Her blonde hair framed her startling blue eyes but also something new—her brightly glowing cheeks. Phyllis's throat caught in a soft gasp. She knew that look. Jenny stood up and hugged both women.

"I'm so excited about another acting group coming to

Sweetfern Harbor. That means my business will grow when people start congratulating the actors."

"We'll expect arrangements to come into the bed and breakfast for them. I'm glad for you, Jenny. You've really grown your reputation around here." Brenda felt as proud of Jenny as if she was her own biological daughter.

Phyllis fought the instinct to ask Jenny a personal question and felt the dilemma of whether to let her announce possible good news on her own.

"How's Bryce?" Phyllis asked. "I haven't seen him around lately."

"That's because my father has him working overtime at the Police Department. I hardly see him until late at night. He's promised in a few days, things will get back to normal at our house. I hope he means it."

"They can get caught up in their work," Brenda said. "Mac brought stuff home in the middle of the day to work on. It must be busy down there." Jenny's underlying excitement caught Brenda's attention. "What is it?"

"All right, I can't keep our secret from you any longer," Jenny said. "We aren't ready to announce anything publicly yet, but Bryce and I are expecting our first child." It dawned on Brenda that the news explained the glow in Jenny's face. "I will tell my father this afternoon myself, Brenda. I asked him to stop by for a few minutes. I know he will be excited to know he will be a grandfather." She laughed. Brenda assured her Mac would be overjoyed.

They offered to bring Jenny treats from Sweet Treats. She told them she beat them to it and thanked them before getting back to work. Brenda and Phyllis waved goodbye, smiling at the secret good news she had shared with them and vowing to try to keep it a secret.

A small crowd congregated in Morning Sun Coffee when Phyllis and Brenda strolled down the street to get a bite to eat. Everyone talked of the upcoming performance. Phyllis's daughter, Molly Lindsey, leaned over the counter and talked with Jonathan Wright. Both seemed oblivious to the waiting customers until Phyllis interrupted them.

"What will it take to get some service here?" Phyllis said. She smiled at her daughter. Molly gave a parting look at Jonathan and asked what the two women wanted. They ordered lattés. "We'll take them to a table," Phyllis said, "since you have plenty of customers to deal with right now."

"I'll carry them over for you," Jonathan said. Molly handed him his espresso and he joined them. "I hope you don't mind if I sit with you for a few minutes." Jonathan owned a boat rental business at one of the docks. He also taught water sports to anyone who wanted to learn. Mostly he serviced the increasing number of tourists in the area. As the days passed, everyone in town noticed he found it harder and harder to stay away from the coffee shop. "It looks like we'll have quite an influx of visitors in Sweetfern Harbor with the play. Word around here is that one of them is a psychic—is that true?"

Brenda held up her hand. "You'll have to nip that rumor in the bud, Jon. We do have a guest coming who is a psychic, but she isn't with the acting group. She booked a room before they did and just happens to be here at the same time."

"That may put a damper on the festive mood. Everyone is wondering about a psychic traveling with actors, but I'll pass the word around. I'm sure Molly will do the same." His eyes shifted to the petite brunette behind the counter busily filling customer orders. He was smitten, Brenda and Phyllis thought.

Jonathan had something to discuss with Brenda in particular. "I know one of your guests coming in," he said. "Her name is Kathryn Parker. She's one of the actresses in the play." Brenda asked his relationship to the actress. "We were neighbors at one time when we were teenagers. She always wanted to act and kept to her word. After she graduated, she went straight to acting school, skipped college altogether. I'm surprised she hasn't made it to the top yet. She definitely has the looks for it." Phyllis raised her eyebrows. "I mean, she looks as if she was carved like an ivory statue...though with a little more personality than a piece of ivory. I always thought she did well in school plays. In acting school, she met Kelly Reed and Scott Wilson. She and Kelly were best friends."

"Were?" Brenda asked.

"I heard later they had quite a falling-out. Rumors were that Kelly and Scott fell in love. Kathryn didn't like that since she wanted Scott for herself. It went far enough that Kathryn managed to snap him up and they became engaged. It almost wrecked the threesome when it came to their professional lives." He leaned back and took a sip of the espresso. "It must have all worked out eventually. I guess that was a while back. They have done several plays together since then."

He looked at his watch. "I have to get back down to the dock."

"I hope nothing crazy happens between guests this weekend," Brenda commented. Phyllis reassured her that it sounded as if all the problems were in the past.

By early afternoon, Kelly Reed and her hairdresser Carol Morgan arrived. They appeared to be practically best friends with one another. Allie greeted them and while they signed in, Michael came from the alcove to pick up the luggage. They were given adjoining rooms on the second-floor hallway. It was a suite with a narrow hallway connecting the two rooms. Each room had its own bathroom and small dressing room.

Brenda and Phyllis sat in the sitting room and waited to serve refreshments to arriving guests. Kelly and Carol came back down to partake after finding their rooms. The front door next opened to a male voice. It was hearty, and he introduced himself as Arthur Walker. Allie welcomed the doctor who opted to join the others in the sitting room before being shown his room. Michael carried his luggage upstairs.

Phyllis told Arthur she was happy to meet the man her husband often talked about, especially recently knowing he was the one who had the most influence in convincing the entourage to perform in Sweetfern Harbor.

"I have known your husband for many years, though we don't often get the chance to connect. He has told me he remarried to the love of his life...and now I get to meet you." Dr. Walker's smile lit up the room as he gazed at

Phyllis, who was blushing a little. He chatted about past encounters with William Pendleton. "I've often told him he belongs in New York, as interested as he is in theatre. But after my brief time so far in this town, I realize why he chose to settle in such peaceful surroundings. The sounds of the ocean are rejuvenating."

Allie greeted the next guest. Kathryn Parker's face was captivating. Her features were classic, like a perfectly carved cameo, and when she turned her head slightly, her delicate profile drew everyone. Allie gave a slight cough in surprise before returning to her welcome mode. Kathryn smiled, though not broadly. She was groomed without a flaw. Michael the porter even looked twice before recovering his professional stance and showing her to her room.

She followed him to the last room at the end of the second-floor hallway. This room curved slightly, following the bow window of the rear of the house, providing a sweeping view of the backyard and side yard in full bloom.

After Kathryn, a group of men arrived all at once. Scott Wilson checked in, as did Keith Moore, who played the head waiter in the present play, and then Rocky Masters, famous chef, approached the desk. Brenda realized guests were arriving one after another and went to assist Allie. Brenda sensed the reservationist's underlying impatience might be because she was more excited to welcome the psychic and her companion. So far, neither had arrived. Once the foyer emptied, Brenda told Allie she was going to discuss desserts with the chef.

When the front door opened again, Allie was shocked

to see the disheveled, heavily adorned figure who approached the reception desk. Several strings of beaded necklaces looped around her neck and a few reached her waist. Dark black unkempt hair hung to her shoulders. Beaded crystal earrings dangled to touch the brightly printed blouse paired with a long, wildly colored skirt. Allie asked if she could help the woman, whose brown shoes, she noticed, looked as if they had been worn for many hiking treks. The woman also adjusted a worn leather satchel slung over her shoulder.

Her raspy voice echoed in the marble floored foyer. "I wish to interest the actors in some of my beaded handiwork."

Allie stared at her. The sign at the end of the bed and breakfast driveway clearly stated No Solicitors or Vendors. Brenda came from the kitchen to make sure her guests were mingling well in the sitting room when she noticed the strange figure. Allie breathed a sigh of relief when she saw Brenda. The owner of Sheffield Bed and Breakfast guessed at once that the stranger wasn't a guest and asked her name.

"My name is Grace Baker. I create unusual jewelry of the finest beads and shells ever known." She started to open a grubby velvet case clutched under her arm that Allie had not noticed when she first walked in.

"I'm sorry, Miss Baker, but sellers are not allowed on the premises. Surely you saw our sign at the end of the driveway."

Grace bowed slightly and smiled. Without a word, she left. Brenda and Allie looked at one another.

"Have you seen her around town, Allie?"

Allie's eyes still bulged, and she shook her head. "That was very strange."

Brenda resolved to tuck the whole incident in the back of her mind. She thought it was strange, too, and something told her that even if the woman was simply a bead artist and nothing more, Sweetfern Harbor was going to attract more and more interesting characters and perhaps she shouldn't be surprised when some of them began showing up at her door. She and Allie watched as the peculiar woman turned at the gate and walked toward the beach area.

chapter two

In less than two hours, dinner would be served to guests. Allie told Brenda she hoped the psychic would come soon. Just as the words left her mouth, the door opened again and a woman walked in next to a man the same age as her forty years. Tiana Lockser wore her long sandy-colored hair swept back from intense azure eyes. Jeffrey Johnson locked eyes on his companion before shifting to the purpose of checking in. His attractive personality made up for his ordinary looks—he smiled charmingly as he spoke to young Allie.

Tiana scrutinized her surroundings with approval. Allie's hands shook as she entered the information into her computer. She couldn't take her eyes from the couple, who followed Michael upstairs to their rooms on the second floor, across the hallway from most of the actors.

Allie immediately called her mother when they were out of sight.

"I'll ask Brenda if we can both join everyone for dinner

tonight...if we're not too late for Chef Morgan. I don't know what's on the menu and she may not have enough."

Hope Williams told her daughter to do everything possible to get them in on the dinner. Both mother and daughter were hopping with anticipation, and luckily Brenda had already foreseen this possibility. Morgan, her chef, was prepared for extras that night. Jenny and Bryce Jones wanted in as well. The table would have to be extended to include everyone. It would be the largest first night dinner for guests ever served.

Brenda told Allie no more could be added to the dinner list. She and Hope had to be the last ones. "Everyone will just have to seek Tiana out for themselves and the actors as well."

Allie didn't care about the others for the moment. She called her mother to give her the good news.

When Detective Mac Rivers arrived at the bed and breakfast right on time, Brenda was happy to see her husband. Obviously, Jenny had given him her good news. He beamed. Brenda told him congratulations in a whisper. It was hard for either of them not to shout the news to everyone.

Instead, Brenda told Mac they had quite a few people in for dinner that night. "Besides the guests, it seems Jenny, Bryce, Hope, Allie and even David Williams have been convinced to join the troupe."

Mac raised his eyebrows. "They are all that interested in meeting the actors? What about Phyllis and William?"

Brenda assured him they were included as well. "I think most of them are more interested in meeting the psychic. Please don't tell William that. I hope the mix of guests will work out well."

"At least it will prove an interesting weekend." Mac patted her arm. "Don't worry. Everything will go smoothly as usual, Brenda." Mac had learned to accept Brenda's nervousness every time the first guest dinner rolled around.

When everyone settled down, Brenda noticed Allie and Hope sat directly across from Tiana Lockser. They hadn't wasted any time. Tiana carried on a modest conversation, but it was Jeffrey who proved most interesting. He and Tiana had known one another for many years and he talked of some of their travels to Scotland and Ireland.

"Those countries are quite interesting," he said. "Tiana has done some of her best work in Ireland. She is expert in her field."

Allie and Hope leaned forward, hoping to hear those stories from Tiana herself. She merely smiled and nodded. Her eyes often landed on Kelly Reed before shifting to Carol Morgan, who looked increasingly uncomfortable as the dinner went on. Carol sat next to Hope and sensed the psychic had plenty to say about her and Kelly, too. Rocky Masters, the traveling chef, projected a more serious demeanor and sat silently as his tablemates spoke with Tiana. Phyllis hoped the noted chef approved of the meal set before him. She breathed a sigh of relief when Rocky delved in with no hesitation.

William sat at the other end of the table between Scott Wilson and Dr. Walker. They spoke of the attractions around Sweetfern Harbor and the upcoming play. Scott's attention was almost entirely on the Atlantic Ocean and the water sports available in town. William joked that they would have to tell the mayor to tie down all the boats, if necessary, in order to make sure the play went on as planned. All the actors laughed. Everyone talked at length about their experiences in theatre. David Williams, for one, ignored his wife and daughter's obsession with the psychic, and when the actor Keith Moore noticed his boredom and asked his profession, David at last perked up and mentioned that he was a local news anchor.

"Perhaps you will promote our performance, all of our good work," Keith said. His voice held a certain yearning to be better known. "I've been in theatre for quite a few years and have been well-reviewed, even if only for lesser roles. It's not that every role isn't important...I've been satisfied with them. Kelly and Scott are perfect together in this play."

Kathryn Parker chimed in, "As are you, Keith. All of us are excellent in our roles." David Williams gazed at the actress's smooth and benevolent-looking facial expression. "It's as he said, Mr. Williams, we are all cut out for our parts."

"Please, call me David. Everyone around here does. What is 'Mystery Along the Nile' about?"

"It takes place during a cruise along the Nile River. There are a few arguments along the way due to close quarters," Keith said. "As for the mystery, I can only tell you it involves the sudden death of a beautiful woman, a young newlywed on the boat. Other than that, you will have to come and see for yourself."

David smiled. "I intend to do that. I don't think anyone

will miss it. At first thought, I wonder if the newlywed's husband is the culprit."

"I don't know," Keith teased. "You have to remember that he did marry her." He glanced down the table at Kelly and then at Scott. Kathryn's eyes turned greener in color.

After dinner, everyone gathered in the next room to enjoy a choice of various desserts. Phyllis, Jenny, Allie and two of the chef's helpers served drinks. David excused himself when he realized Allie and Hope were in it for the long run. He was glad he had driven his own car. The last words he heard when he went toward the front door were from his wife.

"Will you be doing any readings while you're here, Tiana? Or perhaps you are here for a respite."

"After tonight I will be happy to give a reading to anyone interested." She looked at Brenda and Mac. "I don't intend to charge anyone. After all, I'm not here to promote myself or my business." Brenda in particular was relieved to hear her words.

"Brenda, I believe we must head home as well. Thank you for the lovely evening," said Phyllis. She and Brenda discussed some ideas for the next day. It would be a busy day at the Sheffield Bed and Breakfast.

Phyllis and William started for home. William knew the conversation would be all about the psychic. He patiently drove to their mansion on the hill that overlooked Sweetfern Harbor and made short friendly comments to his wife as she chattered on with great interest.

"I sense Tiana Lockser doesn't really intrigue you like

she does some of us," Phyllis said. She smiled at her husband. "I think I'll ask for a reading."

William teased her that she must want more than he could give her, to ask for information regarding her future. Phyllis assured him he was everything she could ever wish for. The two were as much in love as many younger married couples. Phyllis never dreamed of finding someone like William to marry just before she reached the sixty-year mark. William had discovered a whole new life once he was free to marry again.

"Go ahead and ask for a reading, Phyllis. I admit I'm drawn to figuring out if she truly is psychic, or if it's all just a guessing game."

The next morning when employees appeared again for work, Sheffield Bed and Breakfast returned to normal. A few guests were in the dining room for early breakfast. They wanted to explore the town before rehearsal. Brenda and Phyllis took their coffee to Phyllis's apartment, which she still kept there even after marrying William. There were times when she and Brenda secluded themselves there to regroup and chat. Phyllis sometimes stayed overnight when events ran late, and William joined her.

"William isn't showing much enthusiasm about the psychic, Brenda. He told me he doesn't really believe she's for real, but I'm going to try and get a reading. What do you think?"

"I have mixed feelings about it, but I see no harm in those who want readings. I'm more curious about the relationship between Tiana and Jeffrey. They've known one another for a long time and yet they asked for separate rooms. I've heard they were lovers, but apparently not."

"Rumors sometimes prove misleading. This is probably one of those times. He does look at her in a loving way. I didn't notice anything but a friendly response from her at dinner, however. I don't think there's real chemistry between them."

Phyllis and Brenda often gossiped between themselves, though Brenda tried to refrain from that habit when around her other employees or around town.

Kathryn Parker sidled up to Scott Wilson after breakfast. Kelly watched briefly and shrugged. Her once best friend seemed to harbor a dim hope that Scott would marry her. She knew the two had broken off their engagement, one that Kelly felt sure Kathryn forced on Scott. On the other hand, Kelly thought, he was a grown man and should have thought things through and been able to say no. Kathryn knew how to scheme quite well and Kelly recalled how often she was the one to determine what they did and where they went. Kelly certainly understood how Scott had been taken by her famous beauty.

She once loved him, and when their relationship had soured, eventually the close friendship Kelly enjoyed with Kathryn turned bitter over Scott. It had been years since it hurt Kelly, and she had concentrated on her acting career. In any case, she felt secure in her position because it was recognized that Kathryn Parker had a long way to go before reaching the top in theatre.

Brenda and her staff prepared the side lawn for the troupe to rehearse. They preferred to practice at Sheffield Bed and Breakfast rather than at the park where the play would be held. Arthur Walker explained they wanted to avoid anyone watching the rehearsal in the middle of town, but the troupe invited staff to watch if they wanted to. Long tables were set up where refreshments would be served at break times. The day was cool and sunny. The actors donned their costumes and gathered for last-minute instructions.

Rocky Masters had asked Morgan if she minded if he helped prepare light refreshments. She welcomed him into the kitchen and he noted her nervousness around him as he prepared to get to work.

"You can relax, Morgan. I have experience in cooking for sure, but the meal last night was superb. You are as good a fine chef as any I've ever met. We'll work on a few appetizers together."

Morgan breathed a sigh of relief. Rocky was just like anyone else. He explained how he joined the troupe. She learned that Kathryn Parker was the only particular cast member when it came to food.

"I'm paid well enough to please her tastes," he said. The soft chuckle told Morgan he took the picky eater in stride, but she noted he concocted shrimp appetizers and some finger foods with her in mind. "We don't want to feed them too much or they won't perform as well." His delighted chuckle escaped again and from then on, they worked in silence other than comments or suggestions regarding the food.

Allie secured her desk and joined the others on the side

lawn. She kept her eyes on Tiana, who sat on the sidelines with Jeffery. Tiana focused on several actors and then her eyes swept over the staff members observing. Allie thought the psychic's gaze rested longer on Kelly and Kathryn than any of the others, until she noticed the frown on the woman's face when she looked at Carol Morgan. Carol had a portable hair and makeup kit with her and had just then finished preparing Kelly's makeup. She walked over and sat next to Allie.

"I wish Tiana would focus on the play," Carol said. "She keeps looking at me like something is wrong with me."

"I noticed that. She seems to watch Kelly and Kathryn a lot, too."

Carol shrugged and then clasped her hands around her upper arms as if to keep herself warm. She tried to avoid the looks the psychic threw her way.

The performance moved smoothly. Everyone carried it through naturally. Keith Moore smiled when he saw the news anchor's daughter clap hard at the end. He hoped she wouldn't tell her father who really murdered the lovely newlywed along the Nile. David Williams had promised to be at the opening night's performance. He planned to interview everyone who was in it, not just the main characters. Keith counted on the publicity to catapult him higher in his career.

When the actors took breaks, Sheffield employees stepped forward. Kathryn Parker hurried to go through the refreshments line next to Scott. Kelly chose to sit with Keith and Dr. Walker. Rocky joined them from the kitchen as well. Once everyone was taken care of, Brenda and

Phyllis sat with the group at the tables. They applauded the talent and energy of the actors and raised a toast of sweet iced tea to their success. As everyone began to enjoy the treats, it was no surprise to see Allie join Tiana and Jeffrey, along with other staff members. Tiana smiled at Allie.

"You seem quite taken with me for some reason."

"To be truthful," Allie said, "I'd like a reading when you have some free time. My mother is ready, too. She is the owner of Sweet Treats downtown but can come by here anytime, at your convenience." Allie stopped and cast her eyes downward. "I don't mean to impose, and it's only if you have some time and want to do that for us."

"Of course, I will. Let's set a time around mid-afternoon if you are free."

Allie's eyes shined like copper pennies. She nodded her head several times in agreement. "I'm always free around two-thirty or three."

After the brief exchange, Jeffrey picked up the conversation. His stories fascinated his listeners until the actors were called back for a repeat of the final scene, adjusting some portions of the action.

For their part, Tiana and Jeffrey decided to take a walk down to the ocean. Tiana breathed the salt air deeply. "It's wonderful here, isn't it, Jeffrey?" He agreed.

When they got closer to the beach area, Tiana's eyes shifted from one vantage point to another. She put her sunglasses on and observed a secluded spot where large rocks stacked precariously on top of one another. A family of four dug in the sand at the edge of the waves. A dark-haired woman bent to pick up shells from the ground. She pocketed her finds and shuffled along for several minutes. Tiana watched.

"She seems to fascinate you, Tiana."

"There is something rather mysterious about her. Look at her colorful clothes and those beads. I hope they're lightweight with so many hanging around her neck like that."

"She's rather unkempt, too, don't you think? Even from this distance I can see a few shredded parts along the edge of that skirt. She does look interesting, though."

Tiana suggested they walk the opposite way. They sat on the sand and watched the boats in the distance before heading back to the bed and breakfast for a light lunch. Most guests opted to spend the extra time in town. Tiana and Jeffrey joined Rocky and Arthur. Kelly Reed arrived five minutes later and smiled in greeting. Tiana eyed her closely. Kelly avoided her attention and sat down at the remains of the appetizer buffet but found her appetite had vanished.

chapter three

As evening drew, near everyone in the cast displayed their nervousness in diverse ways. All appeared on edge except Kathryn Parker. Her role as the discarded object of the main character's affection came as if natural to her. She fought to keep her eyes off Scott Wilson, both on and off stage. He stood tall with dark brown hair that framed a chiseled face and he had a fit, tanned body. His facial expressions and vocal skills indicated his goal to improve his craft. Kathryn watched when his amber eyes softened toward Kelly Reed onstage. She scowled and wished Scott would notice her. He should know Kelly was weak. Only Kathryn Parker could totally satisfy a man like Scott Wilson.

Backstage, Keith Moore donned his waiter's costume and took his place in order of sequence in the play. The scene painted on the backdrop truly resembled the Nile River. Keith himself had once cruised the Nile in his youth. Their scenic painter had an uncanny talent at reproducing settings that appeared true-to-life.

Watching from the wings, Keith felt the usual envy surge in him as he watched the younger actors play their parts. On this night, Kelly Reed caught his attention in particular. The leading lady was exquisite. Dark black hair shone in the lights, and when she turned her face upward it was difficult not to gasp at her beautiful olive complexion. Kelly's personality matched her features and actions. She was the only one in the cast who made Keith feel he had talent and was worth something. And yet, he resented how fans flocked to her. He knew it should be him that drew crowds, everyone asking for his autograph.

Scott Wilson ran a close second to her, except for personality. His moodiness could disconcert the others easily. Sometimes because of Scott's sudden mood changes, another actor could easily miss a line or bungle it altogether. Kathryn Parker was not much of an actress, but she could hold it together in the middle of any distraction, Keith thought. He didn't miss the way she stalked Scott.

It was in between scenes when Carol Morgan stood behind Keith with Arthur.

"I can't wait until the play ends. Tiana has promised to give readings tonight to anyone who's interested." Carol's face became animated the more she spoke, conveying her anticipation. "I'm hoping she will have something positive to tell me about my problems at home. I need some solutions."

"I'm not sure psychics have the abilities they proclaim to have," Arthur said. "Be careful that you don't take her words too seriously. Who else wants a reading?"

"I know the young receptionist from the bed and breakfast and her mother definitely want one. Kathryn keeps edging closer to Tiana. Even though she hasn't admitted it, I'm sure she will go for one." When Arthur asked about her employer, Carol said, "I think Kelly is on the fence. She told me Tiana keeps looking at her. It's making her uncomfortable, so she may just come out and ask her about the looks."

The cast had two big performances in Sweetfern Harbor, and the doctor privately worried the psychic's words could upset some of them and take away from the play's impact on the audience. He vowed to speak with Tiana Lockser. At the end of the play rehearsal he hurried to her before the cast dispersed to give autographs.

"Tiana, I'd like to speak with you alone for a few minutes." Tiana smiled when the doctor glanced at Jeffrey and told him she had no secrets from Jeffrey and he could speak freely. "For most of the cast members, the success of this play may make or break their careers. There are many higher-ups in the theatre world here searching for talent. I've heard you plan to give readings to anyone who wants one later tonight. I would caution you to wait until after the last performance day after tomorrow. Some may come away upset, which could affect their acting."

Tiana patted the doctor's arm. "Don't worry. I'm here for a good purpose of my own and I won't delve too deeply into anyone's life."

When Arthur stood up, he didn't feel reassured, but they were all adults and he couldn't do more at this point. He caught Rocky Masters' wave and joined him for the walk back to Sheffield Bed and Breakfast. The salty air filled their nostrils and they spoke of the beautiful town and its people. Rocky mentioned that more tourists were due to arrive the next day while many who came for the first performance would be leaving.

"William Pendleton does a superb job of bringing in the best to this village," Arthur said and explained his friend's background. "He has always been taken with the theatre. I met him and the former owner of Sheffield Bed and Breakfast years ago when Randolph Sheffield performed in several Broadway plays." When asked, Arthur recounted Randolph's sudden death a few years after restoring the bed and breakfast.

Not everyone walked back to the bed and breakfast from the park after the performance, and when Arthur and Rocky entered the living room, several of the cast members were already partaking of the refreshments.

Brenda and Mac mingled with their guests and congratulated them on the success of their first night. Neither had attended but heard many compliments from everyone who had stopped by to chat afterwards. They planned to see the last show Sunday afternoon and then serve their guests a farewell dinner.

"It looks like Tiana is ready to start some readings," Brenda said, looking at the enigmatic woman sitting in a chair next to her companion and casting her gaze around the room. Mac nodded. "I hope they all get good news."

Hope Williams greeted the owners when she came inside. David followed her and rolled his eyes. "She and Allie insisted on getting a reading tonight. If they don't get a good one, I may be out the door." He laughed, and Mac joined him. Brenda smiled. She felt skeptical and was concerned about what Allie and Hope would learn from the psychic.

"I hope she isn't a fraud," Brenda said.

"Aren't they all frauds?" David asked.

"They are just having some fun, Brenda. Don't worry about it all." Mac's lips brushed her cheek briefly.

Meanwhile, Mac spoke to Tiana and told her they had set up an alcove at the end of the main passageway for her to use if she needed privacy. Two chairs were situated with a table and lamp in between. Mac asked if she needed anything else.

"This is fine, Detective. It's just enough to not distract me or the client."

Mac and Brenda watched Kelly Reed enter the room first. Several others, including Hope and her daughter, waited impatiently near the door of the sitting room.

Tiana welcomed Kelly. Kelly made no comment until settled in the chair. The soft glow of the lamp enhanced her beauty. Tiana started to speak when Kelly stopped her.

"I just want one quick answer from you. It has nothing to do with whether you are psychic or not. Just tell me this one thing: Why do you keep staring at me?"

"You fascinate me. Surely you are aware of drawing everyone else to you, just as you have me. That's all it is, and I apologize for upsetting you." Tiana paused. "You must be almost at the peak of your career. Theatre producers will hope to lure you in for bigger roles." She paused as if waiting for the young woman to ask her about the future.

Kelly toyed with the idea of wanting to know more but felt she had finished what she had to say. She did not want to appear desperate, especially not if the woman was a fraud. For her part, Tiana purposefully refrained from saying the words at the tip of her tongue, which were that the young woman might never reach the apex of her calling on the stage.

Next to enter was Carol Morgan, Kelly's makeup artist. Tiana locked eyes with her when she sat down. "You are troubled," she told her. "You already know what awaits you when you return home. Your husband will not be there, but your child will be left in good care with her nanny, just as you left her." Tiana looked closely when Carol didn't respond. "You know all of this because you have the gift also."

Carol admitted she often had strong feelings. "And my husband discussed his discontent in our marriage before I left on this tour. I expected him to leave while I was gone." He wanted his freedom and though he loved their ten-year-old daughter, he was too impatient to let that stand between him and freedom. Carol sighed. She had not revealed her troubles to anyone else but Kelly on this matter.

Tiana nodded with satisfaction. Carol didn't stop to ask for further details, or to think that perhaps the careworn look on her face had told Tiana everything she needed to know. It was only much later that Carol thought about Tiana's assessment of her abilities.

By the time Allie went into the alcove, she could hardly wait to sit across from the glamorous and famous Tiana Lockser.

Tiana reached for Allie's hand. "You are an artist, a painter, I believe. You will study art and become well known for your talents in the art world." She went on to tell Allie she would one day meet the man of her dreams who would share her interests.

"Will I make it to Europe one day?" Allie asked.

"Of course, you will, since all famous artists do."

Allie left beaming. Hope squeezed her hand on her way in to see Tiana. She was told things she already knew in regard to her thriving Sweet Treats business. Tiana told her of her skeptical husband. "He is in journalism and such people can be expected to work on facts. He will come around when he sees I was right about your continuing success." Tiana completed the reading by telling Hope of things she could look forward to in her personal and business life.

Brenda served more drinks and most of the cast then left for their rooms. They planned to sleep late, and Chef Morgan was prepared to serve breakfast an hour later the next day to accommodate them. They had the entire day to explore Sweetfern Harbor and the beach area. Scott mentioned he wanted to take a sailboat out and others voiced their desire to do the same.

Brenda worked with Morgan's kitchen helpers to remove dishes from the dining room. Phyllis joined her and asked if Tiana had finished reading for the night.

"She agreed to meet with one more. Kathryn Parker grew impatient waiting her turn, so I hope the last one goes well."

"I don't think I'll participate after all," Phyllis said. "I know William is fine with doing it, but I have everything I want right now, and I don't wonder about anything better coming along. I would say that even if

William was as poor as a church mouse." Her eyes were dreamy.

"That's a good outlook, Phyllis. He's a good man. You did land one of the best, and I'm so happy for you."

The sitting room was empty at last, and they finished up there. Brenda walked out into the foyer area and glanced down the hallway to see Kathryn entering the psychic's alcove at last.

Tiana shivered when she saw the fine features of the woman. There was something about the actress that caused the air around her to go frigid. Kathryn sat down and swung her tapered legs out to the side and crossed her ankles.

"Your goals must be redirected," Tiana said. "You are sticking with something not meant for you. It is only jealousy of a rival that drives you and hope for the one you pursue to come around to you again. You do not belong in any acting troupe."

Kathryn stared at her. "What do you know about anything? I came in here to get a positive outlook on my future and you tell me this? Do you realize how long I've worked at this career? You have no idea what I'm cut out for." Emerald eyes flashed.

Brenda heard part of the outburst and wished Mac hadn't gone to their cottage for the night. Phyllis joined her. They listened to the shouting that came from Kathryn. The comments from Tiana couldn't be heard, which told them the psychic remained calm. The door flung open and Kathryn Parker stomped past them and grabbed the staircase railing to steady herself. Her footsteps resounded until she reached her room on the second floor. Tiana emerged from the room.

"I'm afraid I upset one of your guests, Brenda. I am sorry for that, but I had to tell her what she came in to discover from me. I'm sure the rest of the night will be peaceful."

When they were alone again, Brenda said, "I think it was a bad idea on my part to allow these readings today. We should have waited until the last day, perhaps. I wonder what she told Kathryn."

"We know it wasn't good news," Phyllis said. "I heard something about her career when Kathryn shouted out that last time."

"I may stay in our old apartment tonight to make sure peace survives the night," Brenda said. They discussed the issue at length.

Phyllis convinced her to go home to Mac. "Each room has an emergency call button in case things get out of hand. Besides, it looks like only Kathryn Parker is upset," Phyllis said.

Brenda waited until Phyllis reached her car and drove off. Then she went out the back door and walked the covered pathway to her new home. She decided to tell Mac of the events only if he was still awake. Otherwise, she would allow him to get his rest and tell him over breakfast in the morning.

Scott Wilson awakened to the quick pounding footsteps along the hallway. He tossed and turned until whoever it was had settled into their room. He had no luck in falling asleep again and thought if he drank a hot cup of soothing tea, perhaps sleep would come again. He knew the one thing that kept him awake was the thought of how he had shoved Kelly from his life for Kathryn. This was something that continued to plague him each time he played opposite her, and in this play in particular. He pulled sweats on and a t-shirt and headed for the snack nook down the back stairs. He heated water to boiling and dipped a chamomile tea bag into his mug.

Tiana appeared in the doorway and startled Scott. He didn't expect to see anyone at this hour. Her loose hair fell in pale waves about her shoulders and she almost looked like an apparition at first.

"I didn't mean to surprise you, Scott. I came down for some tea as well."

She turned to choose a tea bag. Scott shuddered subconsciously. It was as if Tiana attempted to catch his attention. She dipped her own tea bag into the tea cup and set it on the saucer. He realized his tea was stronger than desired and pulled the bag from the mug. He felt the psychic's eyes drilling the back of his head.

He took a sugar cookie from the tray and started to leave. Her eyes were still on him.

"Why are you looking at me like that?"

"You are bent on climbing the ladder too fast in the theatre world. You do not see the real value in those around you. Arrogance isn't becoming to someone as handsome as you are, and as talented." She ignored his scowl. "You want to get higher on the ladder too fast. Because you like to trample those under you, you may never fully reach that highest plateau unless you change your ways."

"Look, lady, I don't know who you are pretending to be around here, but I for one do not believe in this hocus-pocus, unlike some people. None of us knows the future. If we did, we'd do what it takes to get to where we want to go."

Scott turned away but not before setting the full mug of tea down. He took the cookie along. The silence of the bed and breakfast oppressed him. He felt for his room key and recalled the front door code given to guests. There was no reason to return to his room. He needed to feel fresh wind on his face and breathe in the saltwater vapors.

It felt good to escape the psychic's gaze. He walked along the seawall at the edge of Sheffield Bed and Breakfast and cleared his thoughts. There was no doubt he still loved Kelly. He was aware it would be almost impossible to win her back. He hurt her deeply and she may forgive him, but she wouldn't forget so easily. By the time he stretched out on his bed again, his eyes closed, and he slept well the rest of the night.

The next day the guests came and went at a leisurely pace. Tiana and Jeffrey disappeared down to the ocean and rented a pontoon boat in the bay. Rocky Masters walked along the edge of the waters and Jeffrey suggested they invite him to join them.

"This boat is big enough to hold more people," he said. Tiana agreed, and Rocky joined them. When they noticed Keith Moore walking alone, they asked him to join them, too.

"That sounds wonderful," he said. "I didn't want to go downtown, and it's refreshing to be on the waters."

They purchased cold drinks and a few snacks, and the captain of the boat made sure everyone was settled before they took off. No one discussed the play, and Keith was happy they didn't. Tiana and Rocky sat next to one another at first. Jeffrey spoke with the captain about the coastline and its history. Keith enjoyed the openness of the ocean and seemed oblivious to those on the boat with him. Tiana talked in a low voice with Rocky. The former chef pointed to several spots of interest along the shoreline. Attention was drawn to the captain who told of lost ships and early explorers in the region. Tiana paid close attention when he spoke of a section near where the general public enjoyed the softest sand. There were small pebbles as Tiana recalled, but the sand sparkled in the sunlight and seemed to meet the diamond-like crystals on the waters.

They were on the ocean for an hour. Once back on land, few words were spoken. Without a doubt, each felt calm and peace restored.

Mac came home for lunch and he and Brenda opted to enjoy a light meal together in their home. Brenda told him of the reading that upset Kathryn Parker.

"She didn't like what she heard, but neither Phyllis nor I could pick up on Tiana's words. Whatever it was definitely upset the actress."

"Anyone who listened to that psychic woman should have known whatever she said was off the top of her head. She's probably picked up a lot just listening to conversations around the bed and breakfast. She could have told them anything made up from what she already knew about them."

Brenda laughed. "You really are pessimistic, aren't you? I didn't see any harm in the entertainment side of it all. I just hated to see a guest get so upset like that."

"She's an actress and a grown woman. She will get over it."

"I suppose we'll know how it really affected her after tonight's performance," Brenda said. "I hope it's as good as everyone said last night's was. I'm a little sorry we didn't choose to go to the first performance and see for ourselves."

They enjoyed their chicken salad sandwiches and Mac mentioned several cases he was working on. Brenda made comments here and there. "Is Bryce working with you?"

"Yes, and he does have good insight. Right now, he is a little distracted with the baby on the way. He told me he hopes he knows how to be a father." Mac laughed at the memory of the short conversation earlier with his son-in-law. "I told him he'll learn as he goes along. I don't think that was exactly what he wanted to hear, but then again, I'm no expert."

chapter four

uring dinner later that evening, Brenda reminded the cast members there would be refreshments served again after the second night's performance. The same nervous anticipation permeated the troupe. Kathryn and Tiana sat at opposite ends of the elongated table. Once again, Kelly felt Tiana's eyes on her and especially on her necklace. She fingered the Tree of Life on its silver chain and attempted a smile at the psychic. Tiana asked about the chain.

"My father gave this to me the night I landed my first lead role in a Broadway play. He always makes sure I get something special after a production. We are very close to one another and this is the first time in a long while that he will miss a show."

"I'm sure you are very special to him," Rocky said. Kelly smiled her agreement.

Rocky glanced at Tiana, who held her eyes on the beautiful young actress. He distracted her by asking her opinion of the smoked salmon. She commented appropriately.

Tim Sheffield realized he was too late to crash the dinner and so he opted to enter through the back door into the kitchen.

"I'm a little late for dinner, Morgan. I hope you have something you can send my way." His eyes sparkled when he looked at the chef. She fumbled with the spatula that hung on the edge of the skillet. "Or I can help myself if you are busy right now."

Morgan's smile curved almost to her ears. "I'll get a plate for you, Tim. I haven't eaten yet either but will as soon as we get desserts out there."

"Then I'll wait for you." He looked at the engagement ring he had placed on her finger. They had finally satisfied everyone with the long-awaited announcement.

"Have you talked with Brenda about an upcoming party to celebrate our engagement, Tim?"

Tim opened his eyes wider. "I thought we agreed it would be low-key."

Morgan nodded. "That's why I'm asking. I think we should have a long and convincing talk with your daughter. She and the others are ignoring the fact that we don't want any celebrations other than the wedding itself. And we may have to just elope if she and Phyllis keep on like this."

"We'll talk to her together. If she ignores us, then I'm all for eloping." Both knew how that would go over with their friends in Sweetfern Harbor. Elopement would never be a viable option.

Morgan clucked her tongue and Tim asked what else

was on her mind. "It's that psychic who is here. Something tells me she is taking people for a ride right and left with those readings. She upset one of the actresses last night with whatever she told her." Morgan explained the aftermath from all the rumors swirling around the bed and breakfast. "I'm just sorry she booked the same weekend as the acting troupe."

"We can't worry about it, Morgan. I'm sure the actors meet people like that all the time in their careers."

When the guests finished eating, Tim helped Morgan and the others clear the table in the dining room. Brenda came in to see her father balance three plates up his arm and his left hand held a half-full pitcher of water. She teased him about hoping to be paid for his work. Tim told her he and Morgan had to have a heart-to-heart talk with her about their wedding plans. Brenda agreed. She knew she was in for a lecture reminiscent of childhood, which made her imagination run wild.

"I'll be free once everyone leaves for the performance." They agreed to meet in the kitchen when Morgan and Tim finished their dinner.

The actors left for the next production of "Mystery Along the Nile." The bed and breakfast grew quiet except for the few employees left tying up loose ends. Several would return in two hours to help prepare refreshments for the cast. Rocky Masters offered to help out and was told they would appreciate his help but as a guest, he didn't have to do that. Morgan was happy he wasn't imposing and if she didn't know of his fame, he would have come across as a guest who offered to help out and nothing more. Rocky hurried to catch up with Arthur and Jeffrey. Tiana walked ahead of them.

When things settled, Brenda met with her father and Morgan. Tim asked Phyllis to join them.

"You can come along, too, William. We may need back up," Tim said.

He and Morgan explained their wishes regarding their wedding celebrations.

"We hope you understand our feelings on the matter and respect them," Morgan said. "We will agree with ideas you have for the wedding itself, but we must do this our way."

"It's your day, and we will respect your wishes," Brenda said. "We promise not to go overboard."

"Promise us you won't plan anything at all, Brenda," said her father. "Morgan has agreed to give you ideas for how the wedding will go but we seriously don't want anything else before that day."

Brenda slumped slightly in her chair, thinking of the lovely party she had envisioned in her head. "All right, we promise," Phyllis chimed in. William shook his head. He recalled broken promises like that when he and Phyllis married. He winked at Tim to let him know it was all in good fun when the women of Sweetfern Harbor were concerned, and everyone enjoyed a laugh together.

Later that evening the play ended, and everyone returned to Sheffield Bed and Breakfast. It seemed the second night turned out better than the first. Kelly told Brenda there was a larger crowd there and many wanted autographs from every cast member.

"I feel like taking a walk down by the waters," Kelly

said. "Does anyone else want to go along? It's a beautiful night." Tiana noted she fingered the necklace her father had given her.

"It's too bad your father wasn't here to see your superb performance, Kelly," Rocky said.

Kathryn kept her eyes on Kelly, who basked in her successful night. She didn't miss the tears that threatened to spill. "I missed having him here."

Scott stepped forward to relieve the tense moments. "Let's go down as Kelly suggested." Most voiced the desire to enjoy the ocean under the stars.

Carol drew Kelly aside. "I'm going to bed now. I'm bushed. Enjoy the sea air, Kelly. You were great tonight."

Once outside, Kelly led the group, followed by Keith. Scott walked at a clip to catch up with her. Kathryn tripped twice to get to his side. She wanted to ruffle Kelly's smug feelings of success.

"Kelly, you did all right tonight, but I noticed you had a hard time when facing death along the river. You just looked very distracted. What happened?"

Kelly hesitated and merely glanced at her tormentor. "I didn't know that. I'll have to work harder so as not to cause the audience to doubt my expressions."

"I didn't notice anything like that," Keith said. "I thought you did a great job, Kelly."

She thanked her co-star and hoped they would veer away from the subject of work. Kathryn sidled closer to Scott and was dismayed when he moved forward. He wished Kathryn had opted to go to her room rather than join the others for the evening stroll.

"I love the sea at nighttime," Kelly said. "Look at the

ocean liner out there. I wonder if they are all enjoying the cruise."

"I'd like to go on a cruise like that one day," Scott said. "I'd have to have the right person by my side."

Kathryn noticed how Kelly let his hopeful comment go over her head. "I'll go with you any time, Scott. You just name the date."

The grim expression on Scott's face showed no positive reception to Kathryn's comment. He took two long strides ahead of her and struck up a conversation with Rocky Masters instead.

Dr. Walker stood alone and gazed at the waters. His focus shifted to the starry sky and back to the ocean. He took several deep breaths and from a short distance, observed the group on the beach. The only reason they were thrown together was because they all acted in a play. Otherwise, he thought, few would be considered capable of real friendships with one another. He knew Scott must regret letting Kelly go. And the doctor was aware of the deep-seated jealousy Kathryn Parker held for Kelly Reed. He had seen more drama among these actors than ever in the prestigious hospital he left.

Tiana and Jeffrey caught up with the rest of the group. Keith stood a short distance apart and looked around the area. He was astute when it came to picking up details, and this time was no exception. He concentrated briefly on the pile of flat rocks near the waters. The others sat on the sand and enjoyed their surroundings for a while. Keith was the first to state he was ready for bed. Several others followed him until only Kelly, Scott, Kathryn, Tiana and Rocky remained. Kathryn resembled a leech next to Scott.

He was tiring of her advances with no hope of unleashing her from his side. Tiana walked from the group and studied a natural niche among the rocks.

A few feet beyond her, a lone figure moved in the semi-darkness and observed the people enjoying the late-night rendezvous. Eyes locked onto the beautiful olive-skinned woman and shifted to the pristine young woman who resembled a piece of artwork carved by an expert.

They all turned to leave except Kelly. Scott asked her if she was coming and Kelly told him she wanted another fifteen minutes to take it all in.

"Let's go, Scott. She'll come back in her own good time." Kathryn tossed her head and again looked for some sign of acceptance from Scott Wilson. None came.

"Kathryn, can you not leave me alone for one minute?" he asked finally, pulling her aside. "I hoped to come down here to relax and rejuvenate. Instead, I'm more irritated with your actions. We broke up and I've told you we'll never get back together again. Why can't you get that?"

Kathryn stopped and put her hands on her hips. "You broke up with me, Scott. You knew I wasn't ready to let you go. You keep hoping Kelly will forgive you and she'll be yours again. It won't happen. She doesn't care about you, but I do."

Scott glared at her. Tiana watched the episode with interest. Scott was one of the best-looking men she had ever met, but she had been right about his arrogance. On the other hand, she could see why Kathryn would be hard to love. She was all about herself and that was not a good thing in any relationship. It didn't help make her a real actress either, Tiana thought.

Kathryn's anger shifted from one target, Scott, to another, which was Kelly Reed. Kelly stood a few yards from them, still gazing at the ocean as if she heard none of the exchange. Her polite demeanor caused more anger to surface in Kathryn, but this time she said nothing to her.

"What if Kelly suddenly died, Scott? Would that be enough to take me back?"

Everyone stopped walking. Even Kelly appeared distracted when she heard the words. The light from a fishing hut cast a dim glow onto Scott's face. No one missed the anger that flared.

"You are completely out of line, Kathryn," Tiana said. "You need a good night's sleep and need to promise to stop disturbing everyone's peace around here."

Kathryn flounced around. "There you go again, telling people what to do." She started up the incline toward Sheffield Bed and Breakfast. Rocky told Scott he was sorry Kathryn was so intrusive.

"She's always been like that," he said. "We don't match. I'll never agree to be in the same production with her ever again."

Rocky and Tiana followed the other two back to the bed and breakfast. Rocky took one last look at Kelly, who seemed to recoup a little, though she looked shaken by the exchange.

The figure in the shadows of the rock scuffed worn shoes in the sand, as if searching for a treasure.

Scott ignored everyone and went to his room. Brenda greeted them and asked how the walk had gone. From Kathryn's expression, she surmised not so well.

"The sea is lovely this time of night," Tiana said. "We

had a chance to take in the wonderful air and the peace that surrounds everything down there."

"There weren't many people around. By the time we left, we were the only ones on the beach." Rocky rubbed the back of his neck. "I guess I'll head for bed. It's getting late."

"Morgan will serve breakfast an hour longer in the morning in case anyone wishes to sleep in," Brenda reminded them.

They thanked the hostess and went their respective ways to their rooms. The bed and breakfast grew quiet, and Scott stood in front of the double window. His room gave a view of the seawall parallel to Sheffield Bed and Breakfast. When Kelly decided to come back, he would get a glimpse of her when she reached the pathway to the old mansion. He stifled a yawn and then a second one. He decided to wait for the sound of her footsteps on the planked hallway floor instead and stretched out on the bed.

No one heard the padded footsteps that made their way down the back stairway. No lights shone in the windows of the Rivers' cottage behind the old Queen Anne structure. With shoes in hand, someone moved stealthily across the wide yard and slipped over the seawall. Slithering down the other side, a muffled voice almost cried out in pain when socked feet landed on sharp pebbles. Shoes were quickly donned, and the beach was in clear view. Only sea life moved with their nocturnal tasks deep in the waters. Another shape did the same but remained in the foliage until reaching the wall.

The lithe figure on the sand appeared to sway in the

light breeze. Her arms reached to the sky as if stretching in
fatigue and then fell back down by her side.

Scott glanced at the digital clock on his bedside. He jerked
awake, knowing if Kelly had returned to her room, he had
missed hearing her. An uneasy feeling engulfed him, and
he opened his door to the hallway. No light came from
under the door of her room. He knocked lightly on it and
then more sharply when he did not hear anyone answer.
He called her name softly. Scott recalled when he and
Kelly were close, he often admonished her for failing to
lock her doors. This time was no exception. He
concentrated on the made-up bed and his eyes surveyed
the entire room. Nothing was disturbed. Kelly had not
returned from the beach. He ran from the house at a
desperate pace.

When Scott got to the waterfront, his heart lurched to
his throat. Kelly Reed's body lay extended face down in
the sand. He rushed to her side and felt for a pulse. Scott's
impulse was to wail and blame the ocean for what had
happened. Instead, he fumbled for his cell and called 911.

The phone on Mac's nightstand rang and he picked it
up on the first ring. He was used to strange calls in the
night, but this was worse than usual. His face was set in a
grim expression when he hung up the phone and turned
to his wife and gave her the tragic news. "Call Dr. Walker,
Brenda. I'll get Bryce down here and we'll meet at the
beach."

Arthur answered his phone right away. The horrific

news Brenda gave him caused him to throw on clothes and run down to the sandy shoreline. An ambulance arrived at the same time and began trying to resuscitate the victim. Brenda joined her husband and Bryce. Everyone was told to stand back as more guests appeared. Rocky Masters stood next to Tiana, who kept shaking her head.

"I warned her she may never make it to the top of her game."

Brenda heard the psychic's words and really looked at her for the first time. The lights the police set up showed her somber expression, but something in her eyes made Brenda wonder if she was a sane woman.

"She was strangled," Arthur said. He stepped back for the emergency crew who had already attempted and failed to resuscitate the woman. "It's too late."

"We have to be sure," said the EMT. He notified the local coroner, who arrived fifteen minutes later.

chapter five

The scene on the shoreline seemed grotesque. Shadows created the illusions of vast dark places hidden among the rocks. Several guests clustered together and watched the unfolding of events. Officials did their jobs somberly, without many words between them.

Detective Bryce Jones realized the onlookers stood too close to the murder scene. "Everyone needs to move back," he said, walking towards the gathered observers. He gathered the small crowd of onlookers next to his squad car and informed them that the beach and the bed and breakfast were considered a crime scene for now. "No one is to return to their rooms until either myself or Detective Rivers interviews you. For now, please go back to the bed and breakfast and wait in the sitting room."

There was a shocked silence. Tiana, Rocky and Jeffrey turned to do as told. Keith Moore wiped pending tears from his eyes. Brenda noted everyone's reactions. Scott's face looked as if someone hit him with a sledge hammer. His eyes remained glued to the body of Kelly Reed.

"Do you want me to awaken the other guests, Mac? As I understand it, most of them were down here with Kelly earlier tonight."

"I think they can be interviewed in the morning. We can't let anyone leave the bed and breakfast until we've talked with all of them." He looked at Kelly. "I wonder if she stayed down here by herself, or was someone with her?"

"We have too many unknowns for sure," Brenda said. "We'll have to question everyone."

When Mac determined the body could be moved to the morgue, the technicians came forward to load her gently onto a gurney. The coroner's van slowly drove away. Mac and Bryce strung yellow tape around the area where the actress was found. Bryce pushed a few more stakes into the soft ground and widened the spot. Mac told him to ban all visitors from the area, which meant more yellow tape at the pathways. Two officers were assigned to stand watch and make sure no one entered the area.

"I want to know where everyone walked or stood when they were here. I'll find out if anyone other than guests took walks during that time." Brenda went ahead of Mac, who told her to start asking questions of those awake. "Start with Scott Wilson."

The somber group gathered as told. Brenda asked Scott to come with her to the private alcove. His hands shook, and his face remained ashen. She offered to get him a cup of tea before they started, and he accepted. When they sat across from one another, Brenda began.

"I know you found Kelly." He shuddered. "Did you see anyone at all down there?" He shook his head no. "What about before all of you left? Who else was down there enjoying the nighttime ocean view?"

"I didn't see anyone besides us, but I wasn't paying attention, either." He clasped and unclasped his hands. Brenda prodded him to tell her about the others who were there. "I didn't pay attention to them in any particular way because Kathryn spent the whole time bugging me. I couldn't even enjoy the serenity I hoped for. I was angry with Kathryn and everyone witnessed that. We…had a bit of a spat, I guess. When we got ready to come back here, Kelly said she was going to take another fifteen minutes and enjoy the peacefulness." He wiped his brow with the back of his hand. "I should never have left her alone."

"The blame lies with whoever took her life." Brenda told him she was sure he would be questioned further since he was the one who found Kelly.

"I'll do whatever it takes to find who did this."

Brenda decided to interview Tiana Lockser next. She had thought about Mac's words when it came to her abilities. He was probably right that Tiana could tell all of them things she overheard from conversations. It was simply a matter of putting tidbits together.

Tiana walked along with Brenda until they reached the alcove. Brenda asked the same basic questions she had asked Scott.

"I didn't notice anyone down there other than those who are staying here. It could have turned out to be a pleasant evening, but Kathryn Parker had other ideas." Brenda asked her to elaborate. "She was determined to get

Scott's attention. He gave more than one sign to her he wasn't interested, but nothing deterred her. Kathryn was very jealous of Kelly and wanted Scott back. From the argument I overheard, they had been an item and he broke up with her."

"Do you have any idea who could have wanted Kelly dead?" Brenda asked for specific details.

"Kathryn hated her. She could have a motive, I suppose. Most of the cast loved Kelly except for Kathryn."

"I hoped that perhaps since you have psychic abilities you may be able to shed some light on the matter. Shouldn't you be able to solve it right away for us?" Brenda joked. However, she wasn't really joking, in her mind. She wanted to know if the woman was a fraud or not.

"My powers don't work like that. I'll need time to really concentrate on the events. I have to clear my mind and may be able to see something I can't right now."

Brenda gritted her teeth. Tiana meant once she picked up on conversations she could put things together and come to some conclusions. None of which would prove anything, Brenda thought. She felt her opinion changing over into the skepticism her husband held.

"The detectives will want to speak with you in the morning. Please don't go anywhere until one of them does that."

Rocky Masters was next in line. His serious demeanor was emphasized by his slightly stooped shoulders. Brenda noted his receding hairline and thought he looked older than fifty-four.

"I don't usually join in on outings like that with the

others. Some of them can get on my nerves." He shifted in the chair. "Kelly truly gave a marvelous performance. It's a tragedy. Her acting skills were superb, and she outshined all of them. Kathryn thinks she is good but she's no actress at all. Scott is arrogant and a fair actor perhaps, but doesn't hold any outstanding qualities."

Brenda listened as the former chef spilled his judgments of others and wondered what his purpose was. "Did you see anyone else on the beach with your group?"

"I didn't see anyone I didn't know. I wanted to return to the bed and breakfast sooner but stayed to listen to the argument Kathryn and Scott carried on. Kathryn even asked Scott if he would take her back if Kelly was dead. Some of us were quite shocked at that. She went too far."

Brenda hesitated after hearing that comment. "No one else has mentioned that part. How did Kelly take that?"

"I believe she was a little shaken at first but then chose to ignore it. I think she was trying to be polite and not listen in on the argument between Scott and his ex. Kathryn has always had a vendetta against Kelly, and it really came out tonight in front of all of us."

Brenda thanked him and gave him the same instructions before calling the next guest to be interviewed.

Keith Moore was shaken and told Brenda that Kelly didn't deserve to die like that. "She had her whole life and wonderful career ahead of her. Who could have done such a thing to her?"

"That's what we are here to find out, Keith. Did you see anyone down there other than the guests?"

He shook his head no at first and then sat forward. "I

did see someone in the shadows near the huge rocks. I couldn't tell if it was a man or woman, but whoever it was appeared to be searching for something. Maybe someone out looking for shells. I only noticed the figure once and maybe they left after that. I actually thought it might be a homeless person—they were sort of shuffling around and looked a bit slovenly, though I couldn't see much in the dark. Probably a person using an empty fishing hut for shelter. I don't know for sure."

Brenda asked for more description of the person he observed.

"As I said, I only got a brief glimpse. The person was rather short, and it was hard to see anything else in the darkness." Brenda took mental notes. When asked, Keith related the story of Kathryn's and Scott's argument. "It was quite disturbing and ruined the stroll for the rest of us. Kelly looked like she was ignoring the whole situation, but I doubt she was. It was hard to block it all out. Kathryn is self-centered, and if things don't go her way she can get out of hand."

After instructions to remain close by, Brenda asked the last interviewee to come in. Jeffrey Johnson's ordinary countenance was drawn tight and his eyes darted back and forth until he sat down. Dark brown eyes finally settled directly on Brenda.

"How long have you known Tiana?" Brenda asked.

"We've known one another for many years. Her gift is what drew me to her at first. We have enjoyed theatre together for many years. We rarely miss a good play. When we heard this troupe would be here the same weekend we had booked a stay here, we were both delighted. I can't believe that woman was murdered down on the beach."

"We are supposing that's what happened. There are no conclusions to anything yet."

"Of course," Jeffrey said. "I understand the investigation is just beginning."

"Do you and Tiana always take vacations together?"

He chuckled. "We sometimes go our own ways. I am an avid reader of thrillers, which can prove boring for Tiana. She likes to be around action, you know, museums and parties and tourist attractions. She rarely reads books. She does enjoy it when I tell her details of one I'm reading." He paused. "She enjoys social gatherings but isn't one to talk incessantly among others. She takes in more than some are aware of. She is excellent in her craft as a psychic and my admiration of her gift grows by the day."

"I've never heard abilities like that referred to as a craft."

"It's a word I pulled out of my hat. I'm probably the only person you'll ever hear describe it like that."

Brenda then began the usual questioning. Jeffrey stated he had seen no one on the beach he didn't know. "The hour was late, and I suppose most people were asleep in their beds."

After Jeffrey left, Brenda went to her office and waited for Mac to return. They agreed to meet in the bed and breakfast in case Brenda found it necessary to ask someone to hang around for more questioning that night. When he and Bryce came inside, Brenda told them the coffee pot was ready for them. They sat in the kitchen and sipped the hot liquid.

"The coroner stated Miss Reed died of strangulation. It's very early to come to conclusions but he thought the killer used something soft, since rope marks weren't indicated. He suggested perhaps something like a soft belt or tie from a bathrobe. Of course, he'll know more after a full examination." Mac realized he repeated himself and asked Brenda about information she may have gleaned from the guests.

Brenda told the two detectives details of her interviews. "I told all of them they would be subjected to more interviews. No one will leave the premises until told they can. I'll get over here early in the morning to get the word to the rest of the troupe and guests."

Bryce stood when they decided nothing else remained to be said. He said goodnight and promised Mac he would be at the police station first thing in the morning. He glanced at his watch. "I guess that means in a few hours."

Brenda and Mac locked the bed and breakfast and walked the pathway to their home.

"Has Kelly's family been notified?" Brenda asked.

"Janice went back to the police station to take care of that. It's something she is good at doing, though it's never pleasant for any of us."

The next morning, the rest of the guests awakened in shocked disbelief at the news. Carol Morgan wiped her eyes repeatedly before hurrying from the room, her breakfast plate untouched. The others nibbled at their food. Brenda observed the faces from the sideboard where she assisted in refilling coffee cups while Allie and Phyllis served them. Keith Moore appeared. His face looked haggard, as if he hadn't slept at all. He asked Allie for a slice of wheat toast and coffee.

"I don't feel much like eating a hearty breakfast."

Rocky Masters walked in behind Tiana and Jeffrey. "That was quite a night," Rocky said.

Brenda stared at him and realized he seemed to enjoy the unwarranted excitement that upset everyone else. Tiana looked at him quickly and then latched onto Jeffrey's arm.

"I don't know how you can seem so jovial about it all, Rocky," Kathryn said. "Maybe you know more about Kelly's death than the rest of us?" She raised perfect eyebrows in his direction.

"You were the one who suggested she might be killed. Don't you recall how you put that up to Scott when you argued?" Rocky's stooped shoulders straightened and fell again. "You even asked Scott if Kelly was dead, would he take you back."

The elegant face grew taut and turned ashen. "I taunted him, Rocky. There was no hidden meaning at all." Rocky smiled apologetically and turned away.

Dr. Arthur Walker sat observing at the end of the table. He picked up his fork and took a bite of succulent fresh sausage followed by toast. Arthur had not lost his appetite. In between bites, he peeked at anyone who was carrying on a conversation. Allie refilled his coffee cup. The doctor was the only guest who left the table after eating every morsel of his breakfast.

The behavior of several of her guests caused red flags to rise in Brenda's mind. She focused on Keith Moore again when he excused himself. Half his toast remained. His coffee cup was empty. She followed him to the hallway.

"I've been thinking about the figure you saw on the beach last night, Keith. Have you come up with any more details? Often after one sleeps on a matter, clarity follows."

"I didn't sleep at all and have been thinking of the person as well. I feel sure it was a woman, but like I told you, I believe she is a homeless person. I did think it was curious how often she bent down to the sand. I've seen people often scrounge around on beaches looking for anything of value that others may have left, but usually in daylight for better vision."

Brenda immediately thought about the gypsy-like woman who introduced herself as Grace Baker. "Could you tell if she wore colorful clothing?"

"The moonlight wasn't directly on her and she stayed in the shadows. I'm not sure about that."

Mac had left very early for the police station, but Brenda expected him back at the bed and breakfast soon as promised. Tim Sheffield arrived, and Brenda answered his questions. The rumors of the dead actress made their way through Sweetfern Harbor before most partook of their early morning coffee.

"I'll help in any way I can," Tim said.

"It's early yet in the investigation, Dad. The best thing to do right now is to pay attention to the guests. Let us know if you overhear anything suspicious or see anything that may trigger suspicion."

Molly Lindsey arrived at Morning Sun Coffee to greet a line of customers waiting at her door. Before opening, she prepared coffee and wondered why everyone was there so early. When the first customer walked in, she soon knew the answer.

"Kelly Reed was beautiful and a superb actress," said one woman. "She seemed like a very nice person when she autographed my program last night. Who could have done such a thing?"

"Things like this happen all the time," said her companion. "Jealousy, rivalries. It's like a soap opera, all those famous people. There's always as much drama in their lives off-stage as on."

As soon as Molly got a brief break, she called her mother. Phyllis told her what had happened and that all guests were asked to stick around until interviews were completed. Molly wanted to go to Sheffield Bed and Breakfast to watch the unfolding first-hand but knew this was one day when customer flow wouldn't end until nightfall.

When Mac arrived, he and Brenda sat once again with the guests who had been interviewed the night before. He spent more time with Kathryn Parker and Scott Wilson than the others. Kathryn realized she was a suspect in the incident and told Mac she wanted a lawyer before further questions if he suspected her.

"Everyone is a suspect right now, Kathryn," he said. "I'm sure you can understand why we must ask these questions. It's no secret you disliked Kelly, but that doesn't mean you killed her."

Kathryn relaxed and told him the entire incident upset

her. "It could have been any one of us." Mac asked what motive anyone would have to kill any of the cast members. Kathryn spread her hands out in defeat. "I don't know that. To be honest, I don't know a motive for anyone to murder Kelly, but someone clearly did."

Brenda thought there was no more to get from Kathryn at this point. They seemed to be going in circles with her. After she left, Mac wanted to call Scott next. Brenda suggested they get Rocky Masters in next. She explained the exchange between him and Kathryn at breakfast.

"I don't want to say he seemed happy about the turmoil, but his attitude left something to be desired under the circumstances."

When Rocky joined them, Mac asked the first question.

"How well did you know Kelly Reed?"

"I never met her until I agreed to accompany the cast this season. They wanted to make sure they got nutritious meals along the way, and I wanted a break from my lifestyle. Sometimes we stay in rented houses instead of bed and breakfasts and then I cook for everyone. I met Kelly the first day, along with the others."

"Have you ever known any of her relatives?" Brenda explained she asked merely to help bring any relationships together that could be pertinent to the investigation.

"I've heard of her father. He has business in the culinary world but mostly in Europe, as I understand it. Since I am a chef, his name has come up in my circles."

"Do you know why anyone would want Kelly dead?" Mac asked.

Rocky shook his head. "I can't think of anyone in our group that could do such a thing. There have been normal disagreements among everyone, but that follows since we are thrown together so much. It can get nerve-wracking sometimes. But certainly no one is a psycho. Wouldn't we notice something like that?" He paused. "But maybe I wouldn't, since I'm not around them as often."

chapter six

Brenda waited for Mac to talk about those interviewed so far. He ran his fingers through thick blonde hair, and Brenda was momentarily distracted thinking about how handsome he was.

"We haven't gotten very far, Brenda. The coroner found no drugs or alcohol in Kelly. There were no marks other than the one made by strangulation. Whoever it was came from behind her and she had no idea the person was even there. It was quick and professional, no signs she fought off the perpetrator."

They discussed guests and their mannerisms. Rocky Masters and Scott Wilson appeared fit, as if they worked out regularly. Rocky's stooped shoulders indicated either an injury or perhaps he aged faster than most, but his hands were those of a younger man.

"We still have guests not interviewed," Brenda said. "We haven't talked with the doctor or the hairdresser."

Brenda and Mac convinced Carol Morgan it was time to talk with her. The assistant to Kelly dried her tears and nodded her head in agreement. Brenda asked her if she preferred talking with them in her room and Carol nodded her head again. Carol sat on the edge of the bed and Mac pulled up the corner desk chair. Brenda sat in the narrow Queen Anne rocker.

"How long did you know Kelly?" Brenda asked.

"I met her toward the end of her time in acting school. I had just completed my studies in cosmetology. We were ten years apart in age, but it took me until my late twenties to realize what I wanted to do with my life. We hit it off right away." Carol wiped a tear with the back of her hand. "She received many commendations during that time and was a born actress. I knew she would do well in the career. It was everything she wanted, which I believe explains her pleasant approach to life. She was a natural."

"Did she hire you right away as her hairdresser?"

"She told me she wanted me to do her hair for her and stick with her as she got started. Later, she made sure I was educated in how to apply stage makeup. It's an art, since the actors are under lights and the application is heavy but still has to look natural."

"When did you last see Kelly?" Mac asked.

"I talked with her just before the rest headed to the ocean at her suggestion. I told her I was too tired and wanted to head to bed. I wasn't going to sleep right away. I just needed some time alone. Tiana Lockser read me that day and I wanted to think about what she told me."

Mac asked her what the psychic told her. Carol explained her problems at home and Tiana's answer. "She gave me hope."

"Did you leave your room?"

"I paced a little right here but didn't leave. I enjoy looking out the window toward the sea. I love imagining what it would be like to take a boat someday and cruise the oceans. I had intended to talk to Kelly when she came back, to get her perspective on what Tiana had said." Her eyes welled up with a fresh round of tears, but she wiped them away and took a breath to steady herself.

"Did you see anyone walking around the grounds?" Brenda asked.

"It was getting late when I decided to look out." She frowned. "Wait a minute. I do recall someone near the tree line toward the back. I felt sure there were two people and thought perhaps someone was taking a stroll. I was getting sleepy and turned in." Brenda asked if she had heard the others coming back from their walks at the time. "They had all come in by that time. This was a little later. I didn't hear any more footsteps on the stairs or in the hallways."

Mac asked for more description. Carol opened her hands and shrugged her shoulders. "It was dark, but I'm sure one was a man. The other one was more into the tree shadows and I don't know if it was a man or woman. I'm sorry I couldn't see them well enough."

Further questioning didn't shed more light on who Carol had observed crossing the end of the yard after everyone came back to their rooms. According to the timeline she provided, both felt sure Kelly was still on the shoreline.

Dr. Arthur Walker was approached next.

"I wondered when you would get to me. It's a terrible thing about Kelly. Sweetfern Harbor gives one the feeling of wellbeing and a safe haven."

He was completely relaxed and leaned back on the paisley loveseat in the sitting room across from the winged chairs Brenda and Mac sat in. The doors were secured, and inquiries began.

"How well did you know Kelly Reed?" Mac asked.

"I met her when she was a young child. I was the family physician to the Reeds. Her father had just entered into the culinary business. He rose to the top as chef in the same way his daughter rose to her apex in acting. Both had talents that served them well."

"What can you tell us about her family?" Brenda asked.

"Her father Jackson Reed owned three notable upscale restaurants in the New York area. He turned everything over to another top chef about ten years ago and started a private business of his own. He had a partner and they soon had a falling-out, as I understand it. I'm not sure what happened but Jackson came out all right on the deal. I'm not sure about the partner."

Mac asked what kind of business Chef Reed started on his own. He was told it had to do with grassroots movements in organic food production. He was adamant about getting wholesome foods into every restaurant, according to the doctor.

"I lost track of the family, but I believe the business included a cooking school. Because of Jackson's research on the subject, the Reeds moved to Paris and stayed quite a few years there." For the first time, sadness clouded his eyes. "Jackson must be heartbroken. Kelly meant more to him than anything in the world." Brenda asked about Mrs. Reed and was told she passed away while in France. "It was just Kelly and Jackson after that. They built each other up and that's how they got through the tragedy."

"I've noticed you are an observer," Brenda said. "Has anything triggered you about the other guests? Perhaps something they've said or the way they've reacted to Kelly's sudden death could be a clue."

"Are you so sure it was one of the guests here?" Brenda told him they weren't sure of anything right now and asked if he had seen anyone else on the beach. "I came back a little earlier than some of them. The last people I saw down there were Kelly, Kathryn, Scott, Tiana and Rocky. The rest of us came back and went to bed." His forehead furrowed. "I thought I saw someone moving around a few yards away from where most of us were strolling. Tiana must have seen someone, too. She glanced that way more than once but didn't say anything. I chalked that up to her psychic abilities. She may have some insight on it. But perhaps it was just some foliage shifting in the winds near the water."

After the doctor left, Brenda and Mac tried to put things together. "I have several people that stick out," Brenda said. She named the doctor, Carol and Rocky.

"What about Kathryn?" Mac asked. "She had the best motive."

Brenda shook her head. "I don't think the murder has anything at all to do with theatre and its players. I think someone knew Kelly Reed apart from her career. We have to delve further into their personal lives. Right now, none can be ruled out until we know who they really are."

Detective Rivers, as so many times in the past, admired the depth his wife discerned in matters of crime.

Phyllis found Brenda and Mac in the sitting room.

"The cast is determining who will replace Kelly this afternoon in their last performance. We all felt sure they would just cancel and refund money to attendees, but Rocky said it would be better if they go forward, as a tribute to her. Kelly's understudy will replace her. Are there any good leads yet?" Brenda and Mac shook their heads simultaneously.

"You notice details about people," Brenda said to Phyllis. "Try to get them into conversations about Kelly and how each knew her. Anything you can find out about their personal lives would be best. I think I'll ask Allie to do the same, and as usual both of you have to keep everything under your hats."

"I know, I know," Phyllis said. "We're good at that." The women laughed together.

"And Phyllis, I really appreciate you and Allie working all day today," Brenda said. "Pick a couple of days later this week to take off. We'll have a little down time in between guests."

Meanwhile in the other room, Jeffrey was pondering the situation. He was aware Tiana spent less time with him than usual. He had hoped she would leave her work at home and enjoy the seaside village with him. Instead, she hovered around with Rocky or with Kathryn, of all people. She and Kathryn had butted heads more than once since their arrival. Kathryn seemed to resent Tiana's abilities. When the psychic told him she had been blunt with the actress about her lack of talent, he never expected them to carry on a social conversation with one another. Perhaps Tiana managed to soothe her after all.

Kathryn Parker went outside and walked along the paths to the edge of the wooded area. She sat down on the stone bench and listened to the waves lapping from the sea. Once the shock of Kelly's untimely death wore off for Scott, she would be there for him. She realized it would be best to stay away for a short while when she saw daggers shoot her way when he caught her looking at him. Tiana Lockser was no psychic, she thought. The so-called psychic had no real talent. She simply formed opinions from every morsel she could gather from rumors and conversations about others and then read her victim to get the outcome she wanted. Kathryn made up her mind to sidle up to the woman. She wanted to know who she really was and above all, the truth of what she really knew.

Brenda told Mac she was going to find the bead seller woman who had tried to see the actors. She gave him a description of the strange woman who came into the bed and breakfast to sell her trinkets.

"I'm going to start down on the beach to look for clues."

The officer at the beach allowed Brenda to go forward after checking her permit as an Investigator for Chief Bob Ingram. She stayed on the rocky parts and focused on the spot where Arthur described the foliage moving in the wind. The detail Keith gave matched the same area. She looked closely at the recent shoeprints in the sand. The prints resembled the clunky shoes the woman wore the day she came into the bed and breakfast, Brenda noted, though it was difficult to tell in the soft sand. In one patch of hardened mud between the large boulders, she saw a boot print that looked firmer, however. The disturbed pockets of sand here and there indicated where the woman had likely been picking up seashells. Brenda shielded her eyes against the sun. She returned to the officer.

"Has anyone tried to come down here today?"

"A few families, but all were cooperative. No one else has tried to enter the crime scene."

Brenda gave him a verbal description of the bead seller and asked him to let her know if he saw her, whether close by or from afar.

Phyllis was sweeping fallen twigs and leaves from the front walkway and greeted Brenda when she walked up to the house. "Put your broom away, Phyllis. We're going to search town for someone."

Phyllis was happy to give it up. She had learned nothing during lunchtime with the guests and now they were all at the park getting ready to go on for their last show in Sweetfern Harbor. Mac called Bryce and asked the detective to come to Sheffield Bed and Breakfast. He had search warrants for everyone's room. Bryce arrived with two officers.

Tiana looked up in surprise when they all entered. She was informed of the warrants. At first, she started to object but knew she had no choice other than to accompany them to her room where she stood by the door as Detective Jones began the search with another officer. Mac and the other officer went into Jeffrey's room after knocking on his door. Jeffrey held an open book in his hand and allowed them entry.

They moved on to Kathryn Parker's room. Everything was packed, and Mac had the impression that once the play was over she would be on her way. Rocky Masters' room was disheveled. Mac put several folders and documents into the evidence bag. They went over that room twice.

Bryce spent time in Tiana's room. "What do you use in your work? I don't see anything like tarot cards or the like."

Tiana chuckled. "I don't need props. It is all in my sixth sense." She tapped her head.

Bryce hesitated in front of the corner writing desk. He picked up a folder.

"That's my private business that has to do with clients." Tiana reached for it.

"I'm sorry, but I'll take it to the station. It will be returned to you once we look at it."

"It contains personal information about those I read." She started to reach for it again.

Bryce stepped in her way and nodded an order to his officer who deftly dropped the folder into the evidence bag and made a note on the cover. "Ma'am, I wouldn't want you to get in the position of obstructing officers of the law," he said to her firmly but gently.

Tiana nodded, but her hands began to shake. Despite attempts to protest, she was assured they were gathering evidence in the middle of a crime investigation. After they left, she went next door to Jeffrey's room. Mac and his officer had moved on to another room and Jeffrey noted the panic in his friend's eyes.

"What's wrong with you, Tiana? They are just doing their job."

"I feel very ill, Jeffrey. It's not the investigation but I think we'd better leave soon. I must get home where I can rest. This entire affair has shaken me. I believe it's finally hitting me that Kelly is dead. It is too much for me to absorb." She wrung her hands. "I told her I didn't think she would reach her full potential, but I didn't mean she would die. I worry that she had that on her mind. It caused her to not realize someone was coming up behind her, don't you think?"

"No, surely not." Jeffrey put his arm around Tiana and pulled her close. "How could any of this be your fault, Tiana? The words you told her weren't menacing. It wasn't a threat at all. I thought you gave vague implications, that's all. If anything, I heard that other actress was far more threatening."

"I have to get home, Jeffrey. They've searched our rooms and interviewed us several times. If they thought either of us had anything to do with it all they would have arrested us by now. We can just slip out."

Jeffrey jerked back. His eyes grew large. "Why would either of us be arrested, Tiana? You are just upsetting yourself over nothing."

Tiana did not answer. She merely returned to her room and packed her belongings. When Jeffrey came down the stairs, he set Tiana's luggage near the front desk and told Allie they were getting ready to check out. She presumed Mac had released them and then prepared the final receipt. When Jeffrey got to the top of the stairs, he checked on Tiana to tell her that as soon as he retrieved his luggage they would be on their way. Her door was partially opened but she wasn't there. He heard muffled voices from Rocky's room. That was confusing, because he felt sure Rocky had gone to the last performance with Arthur.

Jeffrey realized the officers were searching the chef's room as they had the others, so he stuck his head into the doorway.

"I'm looking for Tiana. Have you seen her? She wasn't feeling well and we're going to check out earlier than planned." He felt foolish explaining why he barged into Rocky's room.

"Don't leave just yet, Jeffrey," Mac said, frowning. "I want to get contact information from both of you. We may need to ask more questions later."

Jeffrey sighed. He knew Tiana would not be happy when she heard this. "I'll find Tiana and we'll wait in the sitting room."

When Mac and Bryce finished searching the rooms, one of the officers took the bagged evidence to the patrol car. Outside, from a corner of the vast lawn, Tiana sat in the gazebo and watched the man secure the plastic evidence bags in the trunk of the cruiser.

Drumming his fingers on a tabletop, Jeffrey waited for Tiana to come downstairs. He wondered at her sudden ill feeling and wondered what on earth was taking her so long. He realized the shock of the entire matter must be affecting her gift and that perhaps she was shaken in a different way than everyone else involved. He was in no hurry and decided to give her time to recoup.

chapter seven

Brenda and Phyllis were ready to give up searching for the bead seller, Grace Baker, in town. Brenda suggested they go back to Sheffield Bed and Breakfast and get her car.

"We'll drive around the outskirts of Sweetfern Harbor. I have no idea where she keeps herself but perhaps she is homeless, as Keith thought."

Phyllis agreed it was a good plan. "We'll find her. After what you told me, I feel she probably was the person down there. But who looks for shells in darkness?"

"That's a part of the mystery," Brenda said. "Maybe she is more or less a recluse and doesn't like doing it when crowds are down there."

"Or maybe she is the one who strangled Kelly. She could have had a relationship with her and used selling beads as an excuse to come see her when they all arrived."

Brenda thought about the strange woman. She wished she had paid more attention to her mannerisms and looks but her focus was on restricting all vendors, especially those looking to harass famous guests, and that included someone selling trinkets on the premises.

"I had never seen her around town before," Brenda said. "If I knew where she came from, it may shed some light." She reached in her pocket for her car keys and she and Phyllis got in. "She seemed pleasant enough and left peacefully. She didn't object at all when I told her she had to leave."

Phyllis allowed her friend to ramble and observe aloud for a few minutes. They turned into a side street and Brenda drove slowly as they passed empty lots and narrow alley-ways. She told Phyllis to be on the lookout for someone in colorful gypsy-like clothing and unkempt dark hair.

"Most of all, she will be wearing lots of beaded necklaces and other such jewelry."

Phyllis became more enamored with the mystery woman Brenda described and suggested they go to the outskirts of town. Suddenly, she pointed to a figure who met the description of the bead seller. She pushed a small cart ahead of her and had stopped to speak with two elderly women who appeared interested in her wares. Brenda waited until the exchange completed and then parked her car. The woman looked up expectantly in hopes of another customer. She recognized the owner of the bed and breakfast and looked somewhat quieted as she waited.

"We've been looking for you to ask some questions," Brenda said. "Do you mind coming down to the police station for a few minutes?"

Grace Baker's eyes darted from Brenda to Phyllis before settling on Brenda. "Why? I'm merely selling my wares as I go along. It's not illegal to do that on the sidewalks here. I'm not setting up shop anywhere."

"It's not about selling your jewelry or beads. We have questions about the other night when you were seen on the beach near the bed and breakfast. We think you may have information about a crime committed down there."

Fingers toyed with draped beaded necklaces. "I go down there to find seashells. I didn't witness any crime."

"Why do you search for shells at night?" Brenda asked. "Isn't it hard to find any worth your while in the dark?"

"The moon was bright, and stars shined in the night sky. Nighttime is the most peaceful time of all to feel and assess shells of value to me."

A few seconds of silence ensued, and Grace Baker realized Brenda was waiting for her answer. She knew she wasn't under arrest and didn't have to answer questions. Brenda was aware that the bead seller battled with her decision.

"I have nothing to tell you, but I'll go down and answer to the best of my ability."

"If you have someplace to park your cart, I can give you a ride."

She shook her head. "I'll make my way down there if you will give me twenty minutes or so. Can you promise me I'm not being tricked into getting arrested for trying to make a few cents?"

"I promise that won't happen."

Brenda and Phyllis waited in Mac's office for Grace.

She told him that Ms. Baker stated she saw nothing, but Brenda thought she was hiding knowledge of the crime.

"I promised her she wouldn't be harassed for selling her beads. I do think she saw something or perhaps she had something to do with the murder."

Mac's eyes opened wide. "What motive would someone like that have to murder Kelly Reed?"

"I don't know," Brenda said. "Maybe she knew her from somewhere. It's still mysterious to me why she came to the bed and breakfast to peddle to the troupe. She may have known that Kelly was there."

"You said she left right away when you asked her to." Mac got into his vein of playing the devil's advocate, a role Brenda came to expect from him. "And you said she left peacefully."

"All of that is true but she is hiding something, and you'll notice that too, Mac, when she gets here."

Brenda glanced at her watch and wondered if the eccentric woman would keep her promise. She heard the clicking of the cart wheels on the tiled floor of the waiting area. The clerk rang Mac's office and told him someone was there to see him. Brenda went out and greeted Grace Baker and showed her into the office.

"This is Detective Rivers," Brenda said. "I hope you had time to recall something on your way over here. We know you were on the beach when the acting troupe took a break down there. Did you see anyone who may have acted aggressively in any way toward the woman who was killed?"

Grace's eyes shot open. "I didn't know she died there. I

saw someone checking her over and was sure she got up. I turned around and started back to the old fishing hut where I sometimes sleep."

Mac asked for the approximate distance from the scene to the hut. Grace stated there were three huts between but couldn't calculate exact distance. "The others get used but the one I found hasn't been used for a long time. I have to sleep somewhere." She fingered the longest rope necklace and a soft sound of shells rubbing together permeated the pause. "I had no idea she died."

"Did you hear words before it happened?" Brenda asked.

The bead seller pressed fingers against her forehead. "There was a lot of arguing down there. That's one reason I started to leave. I don't like an invasion of the peaceful environment." Mac pressed for details. "I heard and saw the pretty woman yelling at the handsome man. She looked like a goddess from the sea itself. Her words were bitter, and I got the impression she didn't like the woman standing by herself observing the beautiful ocean. That one looked like she just wanted it all to stop."

Grace had nothing else to say for the moment. Perhaps she could convince them that she left before she saw anything happen, but it was too late for that. She already told them she thought the woman was alive, so they would know she had more information.

Brenda rested her hand lightly on the bead seller's right arm when she noticed the shudder. "Can I get you something to drink? I'm sure there is hot tea or coffee, or perhaps a cold drink?"

"A drink of cold water would be fine," Grace said. Brenda left to get it for her.

Phyllis felt mesmerized with the woman, who seemed to withdraw from her and Mac. She probably would have curled up into a ball if possible, Phyllis thought. Mac sensed what Brenda had promised him. Without a doubt, this woman saw the crime that unfolded before her eyes. He was sure Grace Baker knew the actress died at the scene.

"Miss Baker," he said, "you stated you thought the woman was alive when someone bent over her. Did you see her get up and walk away?"

Grace nodded several times. She took the glass of ice water from Brenda and thanked her.

"How could a dead person get up and walk away?" Mac held his eyes on the bead seller. "Did you have anything to do with her murder?"

Her hands clenched the cold glass until Brenda feared she would break it in half. "I didn't kill anyone. I can't say anything else." Her hands shook when she attempted to set the glass on the edge of Mac's desk. "I have nothing else to tell you because I don't know anything else."

Brenda couldn't let her go yet. They may never get her back. She could easily return to wherever she came from in the first place.

"Will you go with me back to the beach now? I want to see where you spend some of your nights." Grace hesitated. "I just need to get a fuller picture in my mind," Brenda said. Grace finally agreed.

Mac took Brenda aside and gave her several suggestions for more questioning of the bead seller. Phyllis

84

took Grace to the car and reassured her they just wanted information she may have.

"Kelly Reed was well liked," Phyllis said. "Everyone wants to find whoever killed her. No one believes you had anything to do with it, but I do hope you tell Brenda all you know."

Grace thought about her words. She feared for her life if she told everything she witnessed that night. The graceful woman who slumped so easily to the ground had plagued her day and night since the incident. The eyes that looked her way would never be forgotten. She wasn't sure if the killer saw her or not, but she couldn't take chances. The dilemma whether to tell everything or not was an impossible one to come to terms with.

Detective Bryce Jones joined Mac after the women left. He laid out several folders.

"The one on top belongs to the psychic staying at Sheffield. There are handwritten notes you may be interested in. The other folders came from Rocky Masters' room and that information concerns business dealings he has. I noticed some are legal papers as if in preparation to present to a court or to a lawyer, possibly. And this is a diary kept by Carol Morgan. I thumbed through it briefly. It's mostly about her troubles at home." Bryce shuffled to the bottom of the pile. "This envelope contains a contract that was taken from Kathryn Parker's room."

Mac opened it and read through the two-page contract. It looked as if the failing actress was given a lead role at last. There was no specific play indicated but apparently the next one that came along would be hers. No other actors were mentioned, and Mac wondered if Kathryn was meant to replace Kelly Reed in leading roles.

"Are there names on any of the business papers from Rocky's room other than his?"

Bryce opened the folder he felt was important and pushed it toward Mac. Rocky Masters was listed as co-owner of a culinary business named *R & M Culinary School*.

"Keep going, Mac, and you will see in the following pages a possible connection in the murder of Kelly Reed."

After a few minutes, the lead detective leaned back in his chair and gave a low whistle. "Let's get back to the bed and breakfast. I'll go ahead while you gather at least four officers. I want to get there before the guests leave."

Mac arrived just in time to see Jeffrey slam the trunk lid of their rental car. Tiana settled into the front seat. Mac told them to both get out and come back inside. The troupe arrived in time to see several patrol cars speed up the driveway. All guests were halted at the front door and told they could either go to their rooms or into the sitting room.

"Wait until further notice," Bryce said. "No one is to leave before we say you can."

Mac called Brenda on her cell phone and told her to gather as much as possible from Grace Baker and head back to the bed and breakfast. He told her about the discoveries he and Bryce made about some of their guests.

"You can tell Grace Baker that she has nothing to fear and tell her why. It should make her tell everything she knows."

Keith sat next to Kathryn in the sitting room. Tiana and Jeffrey joined them. Tiana said nothing, but Jeffrey expressed disappointment that they weren't allowed to leave as planned. Kathryn smirked.

"Maybe they suspect you of killing Kelly. Isn't that why we're all stuck here?"

"We certainly didn't kill her," Tiana said.

"As a psychic, you must know who did it," Keith said.

"I've been so rattled over the entire matter I can't begin to read into any of it."

"Maybe that's because you aren't a real psychic. You read me wrong for sure," Kathryn said. "I think my day is coming when I'll have the lead role I deserve in a play."

Jeffrey and Keith stared at her. Both wondered if they sat with a killer but had no comment. Jeffrey edged closer to Tiana and patted her arm. He hoped their ordeal would end soon so they could finally put the entire weekend in the past.

Down on the sandy shoreline, Brenda, Phyllis and Grace passed the third hut and arrived at a fourth one that was as Grace told them. It was in need of drastic repair. A few shells rested in a pile next to the dilapidated door. A small three-legged stool was set to the right of the cluster.

"I often sit there and thread the shells or beads. The ocean sounds are soothing, and I do better work here." Brenda passed Mac's message to her and told her why she could now talk freely about the night she witnessed the murder of the actress.

The woman looked around sorrowfully before she began to speak. "I have a good sense when it comes to reading people. I'm no psychic like that woman proclaims she is. She showed her true colors that night, faking her abilities. I can look at someone and know if they are good or not. It's like I knew right away when I came into your bed and breakfast and saw you and that young girl behind the desk. Both of you are genuine people and I knew that right away." Brenda waited for her to move on to the matter at hand. "Take that porcelain-faced woman who argued with that nice man. She's self-centered and has no regard for anyone other than herself. I saw deep sadness in the man. He looked at the woman watching the sea and I observed sadness in him. It was as if he lost something or someone precious to him."

Phyllis and Brenda exchanged quick glances. Brenda realized to get to the real meat of the issue, she must hear the woman out. Perhaps her insight would be pertinent in more ways than one. Phyllis hoped she would hurry the story along.

"I think you read those personalities correctly," Brenda said.

"There were two men I didn't trust at all," Grace said. "The one named Rocky...he was arrogant. He was definitely unhappy to be with the rest and I think he was ready to stomp off and leave them. I saw anger in him. He turned and came back to listen to the argument the porcelain one had with the sad man. She was the one who asked him, if the dreamy woman was dead, would he come back to her. I could tell she wanted to kill the other girl, but others were there and that was impossible, wasn't it?"

"Who else didn't you trust?" Phyllis asked.

"There was one man I believe I heard called Keith or Kevin, perhaps. He definitely acted like he felt sorry for the dreamy woman, but he didn't care about any of them.

I've heard over the years that actors and actresses have big egos and generally don't get along well with one another in the best or the worst of times."

The bead seller picked up a dry piece of reed on the floor and swished it back and forth as if searching for more shells. She looked at Brenda. "You are a patient woman. I felt it important to give you my observations. That woman who claims to have psychic powers doesn't at all. She is a wolf in sheep's clothing. And, she is in love with that angry one who started to leave the others and changed his mind. She called him Rocky. What kind of name is that?"

Brenda had no comment. "What exactly did you witness, Grace?"

Tears threatened to spill from her eyelids and she wiped them away. "She was so beautiful and peaceful looking. She was glad when everyone left. I could tell in the way she swayed in her last dance on the sand. She reached for the starry sky and tossed her head back and laughed. She was happy."

Brenda became anxious to get back to Sheffield Bed and Breakfast, but she was too close to getting the needed information.

"You are losing your patience now," Grace said. "I don't blame you." She looked at the Atlantic Ocean. "I watched her for a few minutes. We were the only two down here until I heard whispers coming from over there." She pointed to the pathway yards from where Kelly's body was found. "I hunkered down. It was too late for me to leave. I didn't want to be seen or heard and so I waited and watched. A man and a woman kept to the edge of the seawall and sneaked up behind her. They waited until she stopped dancing and faced the ocean again. The woman stayed in the background. I saw the man pull something from his back pocket. I wanted to cry out a warning but it all happened so fast. Besides, both of us would be dead if I had done that. The man was quick, and she didn't even have time to struggle much. He had something long and soft around her neck…it strangled all breath from her and I only heard a few short gasps before she went completely limp."

Grace wiped another tear away. "Even the seagulls awakened on the sand. They knew something dreadful had happened. The woman joined the man, and both looked down at the lifeless figure. The man knelt down on one knee and felt for a pulse and found none. He looked all around the beach as if to make sure no one saw what he had done." Grace shivered. "I was sure he looked right at me. I can't be sure yet that he didn't see me, but I guess if he did, he would have killed me, too."

"Describe the man and woman, Grace, and we'll be finished here."

The three women said nothing after hearing the bead seller tell in detail the features and statures of the culprits. Brenda told Grace she could stay the night in the hut if she wanted but to not cross into the crime scene. The sorrowful woman wrapped herself up in her ratty sweater and seemed to collapse into herself. Having told her story, there was hardly anything left to the poor creature but a husk who wished to be ignored and forgotten.

Phyllis and Brenda had no words on their way back to Sheffield Bed and Breakfast. Fatigue wrapped Phyllis's body when she saw William sitting on the top step of the bed and breakfast. She flew into his arms.

"There are plenty of officers around the entrances, Brenda. I'll stay out here with Phyllis for a while." William pulled his wife closer and Brenda walked inside.

She took Mac and Bryce into the small alcove and told them what their star witness had seen firsthand.

chapter eight

Kathryn stood up and glared at Keith. "I think you are the one who did it. You didn't like Kelly any more than I did. Neither of us deserved lowly roles while she got the good ones. Scott lorded over you, Keith, didn't he?"

Jeffrey stood abruptly. "Stop all the accusing. No one in this room is a murderer. The police will get to the bottom of it. In fact, I think they already have proof of who did it." Kathryn stopped in her tracks and asked what made him so sure. "It stands to reason. Why else are there so many cops around here right now? They know who did it and will soon have an arrest and we can all be on our way again. It was one of us staying here, since the beach was empty except for a few of us."

Dr. Arthur Walker walked into the room. "I'm all packed up. I hope this comes to an end soon. I plan to enjoy my week before we get on the road again." Arthur acted as if he was joining nothing more than a lively party underway in the sitting room. Everyone looked at him in shock, but he did not seem to register their expressions. He poured a glass of iced tea from the sideboard and asked if anyone wanted something to drink. All declined.

"You don't seem too worried, Arthur," Keith said.

"I have nothing to worry about at all. Only the one who committed the murder should be concerned, and it's not me."

Upstairs, Rocky sat in his room and thought about the contracts and other papers he brought to go over for the last time before heading to court to take back what was rightfully his. When he had been told they were taken as evidence and were being held at the precinct, he became angry. Detective Rivers told him they were part of the investigation and he would have them back in time for his court hearing in two weeks' time in New York.

This didn't satisfy Rocky. He hated traveling with the simpering cast members who bickered with one another constantly. He looked out the window and watched several birds helping themselves at bird feeders along the pathway gardens. The little birds sniped and pecked at each other, trying to get the best morsels for themselves and keep every rival bird away from the choicest seeds. He saw the beautiful little birds were exactly like the greedy actors.

When he booked the troupe for this stay, Rocky convinced them Sheffield Bed and Breakfast was the perfect hotel for them while in Sweetfern Harbor. Jeffrey mentioned the other historic hotel at the edge of town but Rocky persuaded them, stating Sheffield served top-notch food. He had been a well-known chef, and everyone bowed to his culinary tastes, and they certainly weren't disappointed. But even the food and the surroundings could not make up for what a sorry bunch of strivers they all were. And it had ended in murder. It boiled his blood and he steamed as he paced his room in silence.

Downstairs, Tiana walked a few steps away from the others. "I think I'll take a walk if they'll allow me outside," she said. Jeffrey offered to accompany her, but she declined.

Mac came from the passageway and told her no one was allowed outside. "Please wait somewhere inside. We won't be much longer." Tiana looked disheartened but returned to her seat, sipping at a glass of iced tea.

The detective approached the nearby officer. He told him to stick near the people in the sitting room. It bothered Mac that most of them seemed more eager to escape than to mourn the loss of a fellow actor who had met her tragic death.

Mac went upstairs and knocked on Rocky's door and asked him to join the others downstairs. Rocky appeared to be stifling annoyance as he quickly obeyed the detective's request.

Scott Wilson emerged from his room, too. His eyes were red, and appearance rumpled. When he was told everyone was to gather downstairs, he went back and combed his hair and put on a fresh shirt. Carol Morgan sat on a settee at the end of the hall, gazing out the window in silence. Mac requested she join the rest. She rose and dabbed at her tears with a tissue before descending the stairs, still in silence.

In the kitchen, Chef Morgan stirred a chicken and

noodle dish on the stove. Tim Sheffield sat on a stool at the baker's table nearby.

"I hope they've found out whoever committed the murder," Morgan said. "I don't know how many will be around here for a light supper so I'm adding to the stew."

"I think Mac and Brenda have a good idea who did it. They just have to have proof and then they can arrest whoever the killer is. Once everyone is released, you'll be feeding the usual crowd." His eyes teased Morgan. "I mean it will be us and any employees still working around here. I'm sure the Pendletons will join Brenda and Mac. There's no doubt Jenny and Bryce will be over here, too. That's when we'll hear all the details."

Morgan was anxious to find out and agreed with Tim that was what would happen. "I have one problem, though. I can't figure out what evidence shows them who did it."

"They may possibly have a witness. That would speed things along."

In the main hallway, Mac stood waiting by the doors to the sitting room to make certain none of the guests attempted to wander off. Just then, his phone rang. Mac answered his cell phone and his clerk told him Kelly Reed's father had arrived from Europe. The detective said he would see him as soon as possible. Then he heard a deep voice in the background. The clerk told Mac that Jackson Reed wished to talk with him briefly on the phone.

"Detective, I'm heartbroken over the news of the death of my beloved daughter. I would like to join you wherever you are right now. Please, can I at least see where she died?"

"Mr. Reed, I am so sorry for your loss. I'm sure we can take you down to show you, as long as the scene is not disturbed. We are ready to make an arrest. I just ask for your patience, sir, and I'll give you a call back." Jackson murmured in assent, his voice sounding truly broken with grief. "Sir, please give the clerk contact information for where you are staying in town, if you would." The phone was handed back to the clerk.

Right now, Mac had an important task ahead. Some of the guests appeared restless, waiting for the next move in the sordid affair. Phyllis set trays of finger food down and fresh carafes of tea and coffee. Several guests nibbled while waiting for Mac.

Brenda and Bryce followed him into the room.

"I hope you've caught whoever did this to Kelly," Jeffrey said. "Detective, I need to be frank...Tiana and I must be on our way soon. She isn't well."

All eyes were riveted on the psychic who paled considerably. Rocky sat alone in the corner of the room and scowled. Mac looked at the guests and began to speak.

"The following guests are allowed to check out with Allie and leave for home or wherever your next destination is." He pulled a half sheet of paper from his shirt pocket and read off names. "I ask that all of those leaving to give the officer in the foyer a contact number where you can be reached if necessary. Dr. Walker, you are free to go, as are Scott Wilson, Carol Morgan and Keith Moore."

There was a shocked silence as the remaining guests stayed frozen in their seats. Noises of steps in the hallway could be heard as the freed guests retrieved their belongings, but for a short time, no one spoke a word.

"Surely you don't suspect those of us still sitting here, Detective," Rocky said finally. Kathryn paled.

Jeffrey stood as if to confront the detective. "Tiana is not well. We must leave. Neither she, nor I, have done anything criminal. We've had nothing at all to do with it."

"I doubt you have, Jeffrey, but Tiana isn't as innocent as she would like to have you believe." Mac turned to the psychic. "I don't know exactly who you are, but I believe you are using your psychic business as a cover for your true identity."

Jeffrey sputtered in protest. "This lovely woman is kind-hearted and wouldn't hurt a flea. You have no right to make such accusations, sir. What kind of evidence do you have? What right do you have to confront her like this when she is plainly ill? I find it hard to believe she is a killer. I've known her for years."

"You have been acquainted with her for years, Jeffrey, but you have not known her."

Mac turned in Rocky's direction, surprised at the man's interjection. He was ready to speak when a commotion ensued in the foyer. An officer attempted to block a man from the sitting room, but Jackson Reed burst free and stalked toward Rocky Masters.

"You killed my daughter, Rocky. It had to be you. You are evil. I knew it from the start. That's why I severed our business partnership. I never should have let her travel with you."

Rocky stood up and loomed an inch over the distraught man. "You didn't sever our business, old man. You stole the business from me. It was everything I worked hard for all my life and you knew how much it meant to me." Although Rocky was the one who stood and spoke with fire in his eyes, it was Tiana's face that shone with tears and true heartbreak in that moment, curiously. Rocky continued staring down into the face of Mr. Reed. "I cherished that business. I bled for it. And then you ripped it away from me, like the privileged rich snob you truly are. You're exactly the same as your daughter. You deserved to lose something the way I lost something. She deserved to die."

Mac and the officer caught Rocky's arm just as it swung forward toward the intended target. Handcuffs were snapped onto both men as the father snarled and attempted to claw forward to reach the chef.

"There you have it, Detective. Rocky has all but admitted he is the killer. Tiana had nothing to do with any of it." Jeffrey started to take Tiana's hand. She pulled back.

"Oh, Jeffrey, you don't see anything right before your eyes, do you?" Her voice rang with distress, but a new note of disdain crept into her tone as she looked over at Jeffrey, a coldness in her eyes. "I've enjoyed our... companionship over the years. It's served its purpose more than once for me. What you're plainly too blind to see is that Rocky and I have been involved for a long, long time. We've known one another for years. I was one of his first apprentices in his restaurant in New York. We have been lovers ever since that time. He worked hard and climbed the ladder to the top. Which is more than you have done, Jeffrey," she spat viciously.

Tiana ignored the shocked look on his face. She stood up and faced Jackson Reed.

"You deserved to lose your daughter! You cheated Rocky and me out of an early retirement from a thriving business. We were going to move somewhere safe and warm and quiet, like a nice life on the Mediterranean. He's right. You did steal all that from him, and more. If you had 'severed ties' as you put it, he would have gotten his rightful profits."

Mac directed another officer to handcuff Tiana. "You're an accessory to murder, miss. Take both of them to the police station and book them. I'll be down later."

Mac watched Kathryn, who stood by the window, facing the whole episode in quiet stillness. He approached her and told her she was free to leave for now but must be available for further police interviews. The young woman nodded but did not speak, gazing around at the people she thought she knew. Kathryn slowly walked from the room and left the chaos of the confrontation behind.

Mac released Jackson Reed from his handcuffs as the man had apologized for his outburst of violence and began to sag as tears came over his face again. Mac asked him if he wanted something to eat from the tray. He refused, and Mac told him to meet him at the police station in half an hour. The man sat heavily on the sofa and leaned his head down into his hands.

Kathryn Parker stood in the foyer and watched the fraudulent psychic and disgruntled, murderous chef be escorted to the two patrol cars. For the first time since she received the document that stated she would have the next lead role, Kathryn wondered who exactly put the deal together. She decided to wait for the phone call once she returned back home. Surely then she would get details of the play she landed a lead role in, and then she could decide if she would choose to accept it. She wondered, why not accept the role? But then, nothing seemed quite predictable anymore.

Keith Moore drove his rental car to the airport and purchased a ticket to the Bahamas. There he planned to write a letter stating he was leaving the troupe and all other acting opportunities. He had enough money saved to live comfortably for a year. By that time, he would settle under the sun and perhaps open a tiki bar or something similar. He needed a complete change in his lifestyle, and no better lure existed than deep blue waters and sandy beaches.

Dr. Arthur Walker decided to stick with the remnants of the cast. Demands were less on him and there were plenty of actors looking for jobs. The troupe would once again build up and life would go forward. He waited by his car in the parking lot for Carol Morgan. He hugged her and assisted her into the car before they drove off together.

Jeffrey Johnson sat alone in the sitting room, distraught and abandoned by the woman who he thought he knew and who he thought loved him. Phyllis attempted small talk, but he didn't respond. She removed the dishes and leftover food and loaded the cart. She was ready to push it to the kitchen when he finally spoke.

"Tiana had nothing to do with any of it. She doesn't have an evil streak in her."

Phyllis kept her hands on the cart and turned to him. The man was in deep denial. "She admitted she was in on it with Rocky. The two of them were seen by a witness during the crime."

Jeffrey jerked to reality. "She was under duress admitting something like that. Rocky was sitting right there, and he can be intimidating. Tiana didn't feel well and that's why we were leaving earlier than planned." He wrung his hands. "If she had been in love with Rocky, I would have known it…we've been through so much over the years we've traveled together."

Phyllis decided Jeffrey's assessment of Tiana wasn't going to waver. Even an admission of guilt didn't do anything to change his devotion to the woman. She looked at him with sympathy and simply rolled the cart into the kitchen and began loading the dishwasher.

"That simmering stew smells delicious, Morgan." Phyllis watched Tim scoop a spoonful from the bowl in front of him. He winked at Phyllis and told her how good it tasted. Morgan handed her a bowl and Phyllis realized how hungry she was.

"I don't hear much coming from the other room," Morgan said. "I presume they've arrested someone."

Phyllis told them what had happened. "There is still a lot to hear when it comes to details and explanations. Kelly's father arrived, and that sure added to the turmoil going on." She told them what little she'd picked up from the scuffle between Rocky and Jackson Reed.

Tim shook his head. "Are you saying Mr. Reed stole from his partner Rocky, who then killed his daughter in revenge?"

"It sounds that way," Phyllis said.

Brenda went into the kitchen to tell Morgan there would be no extra guests for the light supper. "We should all be back around six-thirty or so. If you need to leave, please feel free to do so. We can finish up here."

"No one is leaving," Tim said. "We want to hear everything. Just don't make us wait too long for that stew." Brenda eyed her father's empty bowl.

"It looks like you've gotten a head start, Dad, but we won't be late."

Brenda laughed and met William on his way in, heading into the kitchen looking for Phyllis. She hoped there would be enough of the stew left by the time she got back. When Brenda passed the sitting room, she stopped when she saw Jeffrey Johnson sitting alone. She asked if he needed help with his luggage. He realized where he was and told her he was ready to check out.

"Our luggage is in the car already. I'll wait at the police station for Tiana to be released and then we'll be on our way."

Brenda didn't comment and waited until he walked slowly down the front steps and then drove off the premises. His demeanor told her that it would be a long time before he was ready to accept what had truly been revealed that day.

Brenda was startled to realize that Allie sat quietly behind the desk, her eyes wide. She appeared to be trying to make herself as small as possible. As usual, the girl proved capable in an emergency. "Allie, you did great. I'm sorry you had to witness all this. You've had quite a day.

Go on home and I'll finish up later after I get back from the station."

"I'm finished now that Jeffrey finally left." She declined the invitation to eat later and left for home. Her wide eyes looked around at the sitting room door before she left, as if gazing at the place where the amazing psychic had been revealed to be nothing more than a simple con woman.

chapter nine

Once the bed and breakfast was secured, Brenda joined Mac in his office. She was told no interrogations had begun. She formally introduced herself to Jackson Reed and Mac asked him if he minded if Brenda sat with them while he told the story of his connection with Rocky Masters. He didn't object.

"Grace Baker will be in soon to identify suspects in the lineup," Mac said to Brenda. "Mr. Reed, we're ready whenever you are. Please tell us everything you can."

Jackson began. "Please, call me Jack. I met Rocky Masters at a culinary convention in Los Angeles a number of years back. I believe…approximately fifteen years ago when we met for the first time. He was not well known at that point. The thing that stood out when we got into a conversation was his ambition. He aimed to reach the top tier as a chef, and he had the ambition and drive and talent to make it happen. We partnered up—I secured the funding and he was the culinary talent, you see. I attended the opening of his first upscale restaurant in New York.

Within a few years, he owned three of them and was recognized by many critics as one of the best."

"I understand you ended up in a partnership with him. Are you a chef, too?" Brenda watched the slow smile.

"I graduated from culinary school and became quite good, but never like Rocky. I was more a businessman, and my goals were to invest my money carefully, bring investors together, that kind of thing. Culinary venture capitalism, if you will. But I also wanted to one day establish a highly respected and admired culinary school. Several times I discussed the idea with Rocky, never dreaming he was caught up with the idea too. The stress of his restaurants and notoriety too, I believe, caught up with him. He came up with the idea he would head the kitchen and teach students skills he learned running the restaurants—almost like business school, I suppose, but it was very poorly thought-out, and it was too ambitious. The whole thing started to fall apart eventually because there just wasn't enough planning. He tried to cross over into teaching when his true talents lay in the kitchen."

"Was teaching something that lowered him in the eyes of the culinary field?" Mac asked.

"Let's just say I don't think he had enough time to do what he wanted to do. I was surprised at his interest in teaching, but I think he felt secure that he was well known and would draw students right away. He was right. I tried to manage the business part of running it all and he reveled in the kitchen side...it all just got so big so fast. My investment partners started to make noises about how he needed to delegate his work or pick one thing. Rocky promised he would hire someone to cover all the work that needed to be done. He claimed that he had everything under control, and for a while, it seemed like that was true."

Brenda asked what caused everything to crumble. Jack told her it started when Rocky began to attack him for flying around the country to watch Kelly in plays. "She rose to the top fast and was good at acting. She reminded me of the same way Rocky arose, using his talents, but there were times I felt Rocky was jealous of my attachment to my daughter." Jackson laughed softly. "He wanted attention, I thought. But mostly, he wanted me around so I could pick up the slack. Because you see, it turns out he wasn't so good at juggling everything as he claimed. Behind the scenes, things were falling apart, but meanwhile, every time I saw my little girl up on the stage…I was so proud of Kelly. She worked hard and everyone who met her liked her."

He fought tears and his voice wavered.

"We can take a break if you want, Jack," Mac said.

"I don't know how I will get along without her. We were very close, and she knew how proud I was of her accomplishments."

Mac resumed when Jackson composed himself. "What caused the final rift between you and Rocky?"

"My comptroller noticed unauthorized withdrawals from the accounts. The monetary amounts were more than usual for general purchases. The sums increased over a couple months. It was discovered that Rocky had been paying a friend of his under the table to take over chef duties on nights when Rocky was busy with his teaching duties. Well, the friend discovered this was a good way to fleece the company, because Rocky would pay her to keep quiet about the whole thing, no matter whether she showed up for work or not. The restaurant suffered, and then the cash payments were discovered too when our CPA looked over the books that quarter. We followed the money, as they say."

He heaved a heavy sigh before continuing. "I told Rocky I was onto his scheme. It was only because of me he didn't go to jail. We agreed if he signed the business over to me alone, I wouldn't press charges further. He was ready to do that. All papers signed were done so legally. He didn't want his name out there in a negative way. He had misappropriated enough funds that I was due his share of the business, not to mention how much damage he had done to the restaurants by missing work and generally taking on more than he could handle."

"Sounds like Rocky got more than just some money for his friend," Brenda commented. "How much is the acting troupe paying him? Surely they don't have the budget for a huge salary, but he's living quite comfortably."

Jackson shifted in his seat and grimaced. "Yes, I believe his friend may have passed some of the money back to him. He had stashed away enough to live well. He cheated me out of so much, I admit maybe I was just glad to see him go, when it was all done, and the investors wanted us to avoid a lawsuit and legal trouble. Clearly Rocky was more than willing to do whatever it took to continue his lifestyle. The friend apparently had opened special bank accounts for this whole scheme, too. If not for my kindheartedness, they'd both be in prison today."

"Who was the friend who did all this and opened the bank accounts for him?" Brenda asked.

"I never knew for sure...until today. She always used a false name at the restaurants and none of the staff could identify her. It was Tiana Lockser. If that's her real name, anyway. Apparently, she was his lover for years. I never knew who he had in the wings but after listening to her spew off today at the bed and breakfast, I'm certain now."

Mac leaned back. "That means she has never been charged with any of it."

"No, she hasn't. Right now, I'm glad she will be charged with the murder of my daughter, along with Rocky, and I'll let the rest of it stay where it's been the last few years. They are both vindictive and cruel people to kill my daughter in revenge. What kind of monster does that? My little girl deserved so much better," he said and wiped a tear away from his eye.

Mac's office phone buzzed. The bead seller had arrived.

Grace Baker rolled her small vendor cart into the waiting area. Brenda told her it would be secure in the corner in view of the clerk. The woman's hands trembled when she grasped the handle and placed it at the end of the room. Mac came from his office followed by Jackson Reed, who nodded at the star witness. Grace stood still, her wide eyes displaying fear.

"Will they see me through the glass?" she asked.

"They won't see you. We'll put the man in the line with other men similar to his build but not too much alike. Usually witnesses find that the suspect will stand out in subtle ways. If you cannot point him out with certainty, it won't be a problem."

Mac walked with her and Brenda to the observation window. The bead seller pulled back and asked again whether she could be seen.

"You can see them, but it is a one-way window," Brenda said again. "It just looks like a mirror on their side. They can't see any of us."

"I want you to understand," Mac said, "that the criminal may not be in the lineup at all. Look closely at all of them before deciding."

The five men paraded out and formed a horizontal line. Grace peered closely. Her eyes moved from one man in the middle to one on the end and back again. When she asked timidly, Mac instructed an officer to have the men turn to face the rear wall, so she could look closer at their build from behind, the same way she had seen them that fateful dark night.

Finally, the strange old woman nodded, her beads jangling. "It looks like number three. I remember seeing his upper body lean forward a little when he walked and saw that his shoulders were bent." Mac waited until she looked again at someone at the end and then back at number three. "I'm sure it's number three. If the one at the end, number five, bent some at the shoulders, I wouldn't be so sure. But he stands straighter than the other one. I'm sure it was number three."

Mac sent word to take number three back to his cell and keep him locked up. A few minutes later, five women paraded into place and faced the observers.

Grace peered closely. After a few minutes, she stated

number four could be the woman in question. "She didn't have long hair like that, but I am sure that's her."

"Can you describe her hair as you recall it?" Brenda asked.

"It was about that color I think but it was nighttime, and it could have been lighter or even darker. The rest of her fits." She looked at the others and back to number four. "The woman I saw had her hair pulled back from her face, so I suppose it could have been long."

Brenda asked her to show how it was pulled back. Grace swept her thick hair back from over her right eye and tucked it behind her ear. She brushed the left side over her shoulder. Mac called for the female officer near the door of the lineup room. He asked her to tell the suspects to sweep their hair to the side in the manner Grace demonstrated to the officer.

Once that was completed, Grace nodded with satisfaction, looking at the woman she had picked out. "That's her for sure. There is no doubt in my mind she is the one who watched the man choke that lovely girl."

The bead seller's confidence increased until they turned to go. Her hands shook again when she clutched the handle of her cart. Brenda worried about her day as a witness in a courtroom, but she would have no choice.

Jackson Reed asked if he could speak with the woman alone. When asked, Grace agreed once she understood who he was. She waited silently after they sat down. He had every right to blame her for not saving his daughter's life. A quick glance made her realize the deep sorrow in his eyes. She thought in sorrow that she should be behind bars as much as the two criminals she picked from the lineup.

"I want to thank you for coming forward, Miss Baker. I know it wasn't easy for you." Grace didn't look at him but nodded her head. "Can you tell me what her last moments were like...before the person took her by surprise?"

Grace swallowed hard. Her voice quivered. "She was beautiful and so happy. I could see it was her nature to be happy no matter what in her life, or at least she made me think that way. She danced on the sand and stretched. I watched her reach her arms to the sky and I heard her laugh. All was beautiful and calm, and she appeared caught up with the environment. She was...happy." Grace realized she repeated herself but that was the emotion Kelly Reed left for her. "I'm sorry I didn't warn her in time. I'm so very sorry."

"If you had called out, you wouldn't be here to help the police find justice for Kelly."

Grace nodded, only a little consoled by his words. When she retrieved her cart, Jackson watched as she deftly maneuvered it through the doorway and onto the street again. The bead seller described his Kelly perfectly and he was glad for her joy on the beach. He had been told her death was quick and he imagined the smile that probably was on her lips just moments before. It was a cruel ending, to be sure, but the moments just before had been beautiful, joyful, exactly as his Kelly had always been.

Detective Mac Rivers was relieved to observe the touching conversation between the witness and the victim's father. He turned to Brenda and said, "Let's go home for a while. I'm starved."

Jackson asked Brenda if he could come to Sheffield Bed and Breakfast the next morning and pick up Kelly's belongings. "I'd like to see the room she stayed in as well."

Brenda agreed right away.

"Feel free to spend as long as you need there. If you'd like to have breakfast, my chef will prepare something for you along with the rest of us."

Jack declined and stated he would be there at nine-thirty the next morning.

At the bed and breakfast, all eyes were on Brenda and Mac, waiting to hear details. "Let me eat something first," Mac said. "This saga can wait."

The others allowed him to savor the stew and Mac complimented Morgan more than once. The conversation moved to the upcoming wedding of Morgan and Tim. The engaged couple rolled their eyes as soon as Phyllis and Brenda started telling everyone their ideas for the wedding reception.

"You both agreed not to go overboard," Tim said.

"You'll lose on that one, Tim," William said. "Mac and I tried that route with these two before and they didn't listen to us either."

Brenda smiled sheepishly. "We did promise, but neither of you has given us an inkling of what you want."

"We just discussed all of this with you, Brenda," said her father. "The key word is simplicity. Besides, there's plenty of time yet."

Phyllis exchanged a knowing look with Brenda. Mac placed his soup spoon on the side of the bowl and leaned back. Everyone watched expectantly.

"Okay, okay. What do you want to know about the case?"

"Everything," Jenny said.

"I'm interested in how Tiana and Rocky explained their actions," Phyllis said. "What reasons did they give to kill such a talented and lovely woman?"

"It was all about revenge in their minds." Mac related the relationship connections among the people involved. "They ran through their part of the money swindled from the business partnership, and when nothing was left, the resentment increased until they came up with the plan to take Jackson Reed's most precious gift from him in revenge. They convinced themselves in the end that he had stolen from them and so they would take from him. So far, no other reason on their part has come forth. They are vindictive to the core."

"Is Tiana Lockser a genuine psychic or not?" Jenny asked.

"She made that up, too," Mac said. "She's also been a cook, a janitor, a carnival worker...oh, all kinds of scams and lies along the way, no doubt."

Bryce chimed in. "I wonder how Allie and Hope will feel when they find out she fooled them. There is no such thing as a psychic."

Mac disagreed with his son-in-law. "I believe there are those who have abilities to see things most of us ignore or don't see for whatever reason. She wasn't one of them, but they do exist." He went on to tell how his department once used a psychic who gave them good leads that panned out. "She didn't know the name of the perpetrator, but she gave a good description that later matched."

Bryce smiled at his boss. "I had no idea you believed in such things." Mac ignored him and asked for more stew.

"Bryce and I have better news," Jenny said. "Some of you haven't heard it yet. We are expecting our first child in late autumn."

Chairs scraped, and Brenda and Phyllis rushed to hug Jenny a second time.

"Congratulations to you and Bryce," William said.

Detective Bryce Jones beamed as he was clapped on the shoulder and a toast was raised to their future child.

Later that night, Brenda and Mac recalled the reckless young man who arrived in their town just a few years previous. Bryce had been cocky and flirtatious.

"Who would have believed he would undergo such a transformation?" Mac said.

"He will be a perfect father," Brenda said. "Did you see how he looked at Jenny? It was as if he thought she would break. I wonder how long he will allow her to run her busy shop."

Mac laughed. "You don't know our daughter at all, Brenda. She will determine that."

Tiana Lockser stared deeply into the eyes of her two cellmates as she told them of her abilities. One scoffed and accused her of making it all up.

"If you really knew the future, how did you land in this cell?"

Tiana ignored her and directed her attention on the one woman who waited to hear more. Tiana closed her eyes for a moment and then opened them and gazed back. She told her she would have a long stint behind bars and the woman began crying. Tears streamed down her rouged cheeks. She gasped and choked when she finally was able to speak.

"I didn't kill anyone. They have the wrong person."

"I feel the same way about charges against me," Tiana said, "but here I am in spite of my innocence."

The first woman curled up on the flat cot in the corner of the cell and covered her face. There was no doubt in her mind that all three were guilty of their crimes.

"Say, you ladies want to get in on a good con I'm cooking up?" Tiana asked quietly when the other woman's tears had begun to dry.

The first woman began to call out for the night guard. If this strange woman's cons were as bad as her fake psychic abilities, it was going to be a long night indeed.

more from wendy

Alaska Cozy Mystery Series

Maple Hills Cozy Series

Sweeetfern Harbor Cozy Series

Sweet Peach Cozy Series

Sweet Shop Cozy Series

Twin Berry Bakery Series

about wendy meadows

Wendy Meadows is a USA Today bestselling author whose stories showcase women sleuths. To date, she has published dozens of books, which include her popular Sweetfern Harbor series, Sweet Peach Bakery series, and Alaska Cozy series, to name a few. She lives in the "Granite State" with her husband, two sons, two mini pigs and a lovable Labradoodle.

Join Wendy's newsletter to stay up-to-date with new releases. As a subscriber, you'll also get BLACKVINE MANOR, the complete series, for FREE!

Join Wendy's Newsletter Here
wendymeadows.com/cozy

Made in United States
North Haven, CT
13 April 2022

18207282R00068